About the Author

Dianne Hofmeyr grew up next to the sea on the southern tip of Africa. Her travels with notebook and camera through places like Egypt, Tunisia, Senegal, Zimbabwe and just about everywhere in Africa have led to stories that have won the prestigious M-Net Book prize, the Sanlam Gold for Youth Literature and the Young Africa Award.

She writes, 'Places yield stories when we are open to their mysteriousness. Africa is full of secret stories.

For centuries the Shirazi Persians and Omani Arabs sailed down the African coast by dhow on the monsoon winds, past Mogadishu, Zanzibar and Kilwa to trade in gold, ivory and slaves. But how did a piece of Chinese porcelain, a Persian bowl with 13th-century inscription, seven strange bird carvings, thousands of glass beads and a coin minted in 14th-century Kilwa, come to be in a place so far from the sea . . . deep in the heart of Africa?

One night I climbed the path between the huge granite boulders to the highest point of the Kingdom of Dzimba Dzemabwe and as I looked out over the moonlit valley I heard a drumbreat from long ago . . . it was the beginning of Maji's story.'

Other Silver titles available from Hodder Children's Books

The Worm in the Well
The Animal Garden
William Mayne

The Burning
The Stones of the Moon
The Spring on the Mountain
The Lord of the Dance
Storm Voice
Judy Allen

The Shamer's Daughter
The Shamer's Signet
Lene Kaaberbol

Darkwater Hall
The Lammas Field
The Oracle
Catherine Fisher

East of Midnight
The Castle of Dark
THE WOLF TOWER SEQUENCE:
Law of the Wolf Tower
Wolf Star Rise
Queen of the Wolves
Wolf Wing
Tanith Lee

THE
WATERBEARER

DIANNE HOFMEYR

**Hodder
Children's
Books**

a division of Hodder Headline Limited

For Michael

A Catalogue record for this book is available from
the British Library

ISBN 0 340 85444 8

Typeset in Bembo by Avon Dataset Ltd,
Bidford-on-Avon, Warwickshire

Printed and bound in Great Britain by
Bookmarque Ltd., Croydon, Surrey

The paper and board used in this paperback by Hodder Children's
Books are natural recyclable products made from wood grown in
sustainable forests. The manufacturing processes conform
to the environmental regulations of the country of origin.

Hodder Children's Books
a division of Hodder Headline Limited
338 Euston Road
London NW1 3BH

Contents

The Scroll   1

Part One: The Storm   3

Part Two: The Journey   25

Part Three: The Kingdom   59

Part Four: The Hakata   81

Part Five: Birds of Prey   105

Part Six: Water   129

Part Seven: Fire   161

Part Eight: Fire and Water   183

The Scroll and the Ring   197

The Scroll

'The mystery of wood is not that it burns but that it floats . . .'

So begins the first sentence, written in small Arabic characters.

The girl sits looking at the way the dark ink fades in the turn of the strokes against the parchment. In the lamplight the writing seems to swirl and dance and make a story of its own. She smoothes away the creases and reads the words that are already written on her heart.

'And so we came to Sofala and built a dhow and waited for the season of the south-west monsoon. Then the three of us set out with the wind piling the sea into high mountain ridges at our back and pushing us on. We sailed northwards up the coast to the mouth of the Great River. With gusts of wind filling our sails and our hull riding the waves as easily as a water bird floats, we sped on towards Kilwa.'

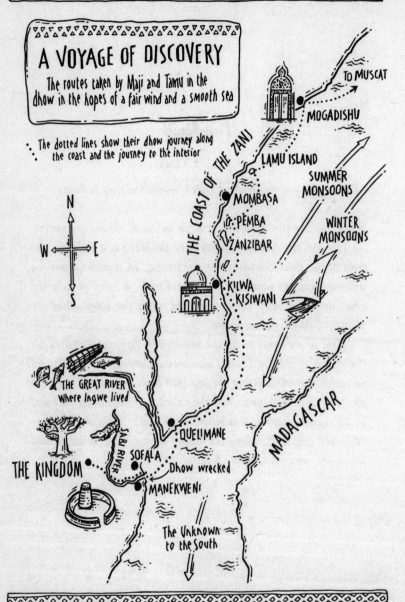

A VOYAGE OF DISCOVERY

The routes taken by Maji and Tamu in the
dhow in the hopes of a fair wind and a smooth sea

The dotted lines show their dhow journey along
the coast and the journey to the interior

TO MUSCAT

MOGADISHU

THE COAST OF THE ZANJ

LAMU ISLAND

SUMMER MONSOONS

MOMBASA

PEMBA

WINTER MONSOONS

ZANZIBAR

N
W   E
S

KILWA KISIWANI

THE GREAT RIVER
where Ingwe lived

MADAGASCAR

QUELIMANE

SABI RIVER

SOFALA

THE KINGDOM

Dhow wrecked

MANEKWENI

The Unknown
to the South

PART ONE
THE STORM

One

When it was time to lay the body in the grave, he sat back on his haunches. The grave was too shallow. It should have been deeper. Deep enough to arrange the body seated. Facing the rising sun. That is how it should have been.

Gently, he stretched out the legs.

How should he arrange the arms? Folded over the chest with the palms pressed together as if in prayer? Or at the sides as if in sleep?

The hands lay open. The fingers slightly curled. There were no ink stains on them now. On the forefinger of the right hand was the ring. It hung loosely as if the flesh had already given up its hold on bone and sinew. It was of no use to the finger now. He drew it off over the bumpy knuckle. The outer side of the silver shank closest to the thumb was worn smooth as silk from holding the sail-rope.

He slipped the ring over his thumb and felt the weight of its silver and the two heavy stones of orange cornelian and blue lapis lazuli that lay clasped against each other.

Fire and water.

Then he smoothed the hair back from the face. In the flat dawn light the lined forehead seemed naked and exposed without the head–cloth.

He slid a quick glance at the eyes. They stared unseeingly past him towards the birds circling high against the sky. Bits of sand flecked the dark irises. He stroked the lids down. Then he picked up two heavy shells and placed one over each socket.

He knelt down close to the ear and whispered the words of the KiSwahili farewell. 'Haya kwa heri . . . Haya kwa heri.'

Then he stood up.

He had attended to each part of the body separately. Trying not to see the whole person. Now he looked down properly for the first time. He saw the sinewy legs lying so still. The arms so loose at the sides. The face with shell eyes. It wasn't that he had been scared to look before. There were no wounds or clots of blood, or anything to frighten him. In fact, there was nothing to indicate that the person wasn't sleeping. But now seen as a whole, the body became the person he had known.

Surely now Tamu would suddenly sit up. The shells would fall from his eyes. He would laugh and the gap between his teeth would show. 'Fooled you, boy!' he would say.

But all that moved were small cascades of sand that slipped down as the sides of the grave began to dry.

The thing he dreaded most was still to come.

He turned away. Across the sea a glow was beginning to mark the east. It was time for the first dawn prayer. But now the words failed him.

A breeze ruffled the water and left a trail of silvery shadows. In the strange light the earth seemed to be sliding away. The air seemed full of spells.

Birds were circling. Very high. Gliding. Twisting. Their screeches cutting the silence and drifting after them. Then swooping in low. Bright eyes watching. Sharp bills ready to peck.

He hurled shells at them.

Now the task had to be completed.

He began at the feet. Scooping and patting sand over the legs. Then the chest. Digging furiously without thinking.

Then the time came to cover the face. Now he was grateful for the shells over the eyes. He began dribbling sand gently into the grey-streaked beard. Around the mouth. Across the cheekbones. Over the shells. This was a game. Nothing more than a game. A game of burying. He clenched his jaw. He dug faster. Sand flew in all directions.

At last it was done. He fell down exhausted alongside the mound.

Later when he woke the sun was already high above the sea. He felt it burning into his salt-soaked skin. From the corner of his eye he saw the mound had lost its dampness. His handprints had already smoothed over and blurred.

He sensed the dry sand shifting. Settling into spaces.

Trickling into crevices. Sliding, slithering around shapes that hadn't been there long.

The sun bit into him. He picked at the grazes on his arms made by the coral. They were crusted and itchy. His throat felt dry.

How long since he had last eaten? How long since he had last tasted cool water? The night before? Two nights before? When?

They had caught a fish. Afterwards they had sucked oranges. The juice sweet and warm as the sun as it slipped away beneath the sea. With the sails left loose they had fallen asleep, lulled by the rise and fall of the swells beneath them.

In the darkness the wind had come like a howling beast. It had clawed at the sea. Hurled itself at the dhow. The waves had crashed over them. Above the shrieking wind he had heard the sails rip and the terrible crack of old wood.

Now his head spun in the hot sun. He needed water. But he was too tired to search for it. Too tired to move. Waves pushed up on to the beach, one after another. Backwards. Forwards. Shimmering. Sliding. Eventually he lost count. He lay back waiting. Waiting in hope of something. Of what? He wasn't sure. Perhaps it was nothing more than the hope of a cool breeze.

After some time . . . how long he wasn't sure . . . the sun seemed to have stopped in the sky . . . his eyes came to rest on something different. In the foam-white shallows a dark shape appeared.

A piece of Tamu's dhow? Another body?

The sun bristled on the water. There were more shapes. Too many for bodies.

He sat up. His head turned in circles. He pressed his palms against his eye sockets to refocus his eyes. But the shapes remained along the foam-line where the waves were breaking. He shaded his eyes and watched while the sun passed slowly overhead and burnt against his back.

Eventually the shapes began to emerge from the water. Dark outlines formed against the wet, shiny sand. Heads poked at the air. The shapes became turtles.

They stopped and swung their heads from side to side as they tested the air. Then they heaved forward again and began their slow journey past him, making drag marks across the damp sand. Watery tears like drools of saliva flowed from their eyes. Their patterned scutes still glistened with moisture. Necks and legs wrinkled, stretched, and reshaped as they walked. The skin made soft sucking sounds as it moved away from their shells.

They were huge and old. Perhaps more ancient than the dhow? Nine of them in all.

Something stirred inside him like a moth fluttering against his ribcage. Why were they here? Why were they on this same stretch of sand? During the storm when the waves were sucking him under, pulling him in, there had suddenly been a feeling of something under him. Could it have been them? Could they have held him up? Helped him to shore?

Now the turtles nudged the sand with their beaks. They began digging with their hind flippers. Thrusting with their tails. They burrowed and settled. They were females. This was an egg-laying ritual.

He narrowed his eyes and imagined the eggs falling one by one into the shallow nests.

The birds made silent landings and stood in a semi-circle. The sun dipped behind a line of palm trees. But the turtles remained motionless on their nests of sand.

He waited and watched as darkness crept in. He was no longer alone. The turtles were there with starlight gleaming across their shells, laying their eggs in silence. He crept closer. He lay on the warm sand at the edge of the whispering palms. In the darkness, he heard the sea hold its breath and listen.

Two

Later when he woke, the sun was beating down again. Palm trees were dancing across the sand. Turning. Twisting their fronds. Waving about like the arms of a giant octopus in the shimmering heat. Strange sounds filled the air.

His eyes blurred, then focused again against the sharp light.

They were not palms. They were men with sticks! Birds swooped down between them. A swirling mass. Two men were stabbing at the turtles. Pinning their heads to the sand.

What people were these that came from nowhere? That killed so fiercely? If this is what they did to turtles, what would they do to him?

Praise Allah, who could save him now?

He pressed his body against a palm. Gusts of wind flung their strange voices towards him. He had heard traders in Kilwa speak that way. If he listened well, he could guess at what they were saying.

They were large men with wild hair. The heavier one wore his pulled and twisted back and tied with a thong.

Skins hung from their waists. Over these, they had on extraordinary cloaks. The man with his hair tied back wore one of many different kinds of animal tails, each piece a different shade that swung and trailed in the sand as he moved. The other had a shorter cloak of yellow fur with small patches of black on it. A trader from Mogadishu had once kept a wild animal with a skin like this. A leopard.

He scanned the length of the shore. The sand was streaked with blood. Some upturned turtles waved their flippers feebly in the air. Birds pecked and plucked at their flesh. There was no sign of a boat. They seemed to have travelled with few possessions. They could only have come on foot. One of them, the one with the animal-tail cloak, cradled a turtle shell in the basin of his folded legs and began carving out the flesh.

'The Great Mambo will be pleased with the turtle shells.'

The words were confusing. If he listened well, there were only some he understood.

The other man replied. 'Before the turtle tracks are lost, we must find the nests and collect the eggs.'

Now they were moving towards him. He tried to melt into the trunk of the palm. Through a triangle of light between the silent leaves, he watched their legs and feet as they crossed the sand. The grave mound was directly in their path.

They stopped at it.

'La!' The word caught in his throat.

He ran forward, his arms beating the air. 'La! *LA!*'

He threw himself across the mound in front of their feet.

But it was too late. They had already kicked some sand aside.

A man grabbed him by the shoulders. The other began digging. Then Tamu's face lay exposed. Strands of his hair lay like curls of faded seaweed. The shells no longer covered his eyes.

The man with the leopard cloak looked up at him. Then he crouched forward over Tamu's body. 'We must bury him again.'

'Why should we bother? This is the one we should be bothering with.' The other man yanked his shoulder and pulled both arms up behind his back.

The man with the leopard cloak glanced at him again. He seemed to be searching for the right words.

'By what name are you called?' But the language of KiSwahili lost all strength in his mouth. He seemed to know only bits and pieces of it. The words were like wind trying to fill a torn sail.

'It's of no importance by what he's called!' The other man spoke roughly in his own language. 'He won't need a name much longer!'

'By what name?' The leopard-cloaked one stood up. He rested one hand lightly on a wooden sheath that held a knife. Bracelets glinted on his arms and his muscles made thick knots across his chest.

The boy looked into his face. His eyes were dark and without measure, like the ocean on a stormy day. He turned away from the darkness.

'Maji . . .' His tongue was clumsy. It felt uncomfortable around the sound of his name. He bit his lip to make the saliva flow. 'Maji . . .' he tried to say again.

'Are there others with you?'

'It's better if he is truly alone.' The one holding him tightened his grip.

'Hold your tongue, Bere!' the leopard-cloaked man hissed. 'He needs water.'

For the first time Maji noticed the two water-skins. His throat tightened. He could smell the water. Feel it on his tongue. Taste it. The liquid thumped inside the bag as the man with the leopard cloak held the water-skin to his mouth. The water was warm and tasted of hide. He drank greedily.

Then the man pointed down. 'Who is this person?'

He couldn't look. No, he had given Tamu his last glance. He had laid him down in the sand not sitting as it should have been, but still with his face turned towards the land of Allah, so the morning sun would bless his spirit.

It had taken courage to cover Tamu's face with sand. He didn't have enough courage left to see it uncovered again.

His eyes searched the sea. It was smooth. As if there had never been a storm. As if the turtles had never swum through the waves. Now they were lying scattered and headless on the sand.

The man holding him, the one called Bere, poked him sharply in the ribs. 'Answer!'

'Is he your father?' the leopard-cloaked man asked.

He nodded. 'Yes. My father.'

'Where do you come from?'

'What does it matter where he comes from?'

'From where?' the leopard-cloaked man asked again.

He looked from one to the other. Their faces were hard and strong as if carved from stone. How would he explain to them?

'From many places,' he said in his own language.

'There's no wisdom in your words!' The one called Bere struck out with the back of his hand. The blow fell full on the side of his jaw. Clearly Bere understood the language of KiSwahili even if he didn't speak it.

'My father was a trader.' The pain in his jaw muddled the words. 'He owned a dhow. We traded between many lands.'

'What goods did you trade in?'

Bere stood over him blocking out the sun. He shrank from the darkness of his shadow. He wanted to be gone from this man.

'Answer!' Bere lifted his hand as if to strike again.

'We . . .' He searched for the words. They had traded in so many things. It was too much to tell. He was too tired. His jaw throbbed.

'Yes?'

'We . . . we sailed southwards. On the winter monsoon. Our dhow was filled with rugs and pottery from Persia.'

'From where did you sail?'

'From the port of Musqat in Persia. Down the coast of the Zanj.'

How was it possible he could speak so lightly of these places? Would they understand the things of Musqat? The minarets pale against the dark hills? The huddle of lime-washed buildings? The harbour at dusk with lamplight making paths of gold across the water? The muezzin calling out evening prayers? Had they seen this? Had they been there?

'Go on,' the leopard-cloaked man urged.

'We sailed on the winter monsoon to Zanj-Bar and the islands of Pemba and Manda . . .' He faltered as his tongue rolled over the names. Names as beautiful as sea-washed pebbles.

'In Zanj-Bar huge jahazis much larger than Tamu's dhow, came across the ocean. They brought silk and cotton from Cambaya. Porcelain eating-bowls and glass beads from Canton.'

In the sunlight of the marketplace, the silk had shone like coloured water and the glass beads had glittered like jewels. This they had not seen. And how could someone understand the size of a deep-hulled jahazi if he had never seen one? Their sails were so vast they drifted across the dark blue ocean like a cloud. There had been one that had carried a giraffe from Mogadishu as a gift to the Sultan of Cambaya. This he couldn't tell them. They wouldn't believe him. They weren't people of the sea. They had no look of far-off places in their eyes. Their eyes were hard.

'We sailed down the coast to Mogadishu.' Mogadishu. The noise and smell of the camel market.

'To Merca.' Footpaths through rustling banana leaves.

'And Brava and Malindi and Mombasa.' Places he and Tamu knew well. Names that rolled off his tongue like a prayer. A prayer that would shield him from these strange men.

'And?'

'And Kilwa . . .' Kilwa Kisiwani. The smooth sound whispered in his head as softly as palm fronds in a breeze. Kilwa of the Island. Set on cliffs surrounded by shimmering sea. The magnificent Husuni Kubwa Palace sprawling across the highest cliff. From the harbour below, he had watched the Sultan and his officers and ladies of court parading in their fine gold-threaded clothing.

'Kilwa was where we lived.'

The house with its cool courtyard and the smell of oranges and sweet figs.

'And then?'

'Then in the summer monsoon we left Kilwa. We sailed north again, taking iron, ivory, gold and even mangrove poles back to Persia.'

Would they know Persia was a treeless country? That the people were desperate for wood?

'There is no place by the name of Kilwa near here! Why are you here?' Bere jerked his arm.

'This was the first time we sailed so far south. We wanted to reach the trading posts of Sofala. We came to find ivory and copper. It's not a metal of Kilwa.'

This they wouldn't know.

'We brought with us glass beads from Persia. Traders told us beads were needed in Sofala. It was past the time

17

of the monsoon but even so, a storm blew us further south than we meant to sail.'

'A storm?'

Maji nodded. 'Between the mainland and the island of Malagasy, the waters rush violently. All the winds and currents gather here.'

'Tch! His words are made up as he speaks! There is no truth in what he says! He's too far down the coast for Sofala!'

'You heard him, Bere! A storm swept the dhow past the trading places of Sofala. If he did not know these places, how could he speak of them?'

Bere pulled Maji around so that he faced him squarely and gripped both shoulders hard. 'If you speak the truth, boy, where are the things you used for trade?'

'Lost.'

'Lost?'

Maji nodded. He thought of the bright Persian beads making a patterned carpet on the floor of the sea.

'Lost? All of it? The gold? The ivory? The beads and the cloth? Impossible! Are they buried here as well? Hidden under this sand?' Bere pulled his lips back. His teeth showed very white against his dark skin. But he wasn't smiling.

'Are they buried with this body?' He kicked at the mound.

'No!' Maji's fingers clenched tightly. He wanted to fight back. He wanted to be gone from this man. But he was trapped in his grip.

'Where are they?'

'All lost! Somewhere in the sea!'

'The treasure all lost . . . except for this!' Bere lunged forward and ripped at his thumb.

'That's my father's ring!'

'And now it is mine!' Bere slipped it on to the little finger of his right hand. He narrowed his eyes. 'Why should you be the only one saved? Where are the others that sailed the dhow with you?' He came up close.

Maji shrank back from the smell of him. 'It was . . .' he bit his lip. He couldn't say the turtles had saved him. Perhaps it hadn't happened. Perhaps he had imagined they had lifted him from the sea. The men wouldn't believe him.

There was so much talking. There had never been need for much talk with Tamu. Between the stories Tamu told, there were wide spaces. Spaces filled with the thud of surf against the coral reef and the shudder of wind in the sail.

'How did you know where Sofala would be?' the leopard-cloaked man asked quietly.

'My father drew maps from what he had seen and from what other traders told him. We followed the pattern of the stars. From the height of a star at a certain time we knew where we were.'

'Tch! He speaks foolishly!' Bere gave him a shove.

For a few moments Maji stood free. Should he run? But before he could move, Bere held up a rope of twisted creeper strands and made a tight knot around his right foot. Then he took the opposite end and tied it around his own waist. It was a long rope. How would such a long rope stop him struggling if they wanted to kill him?

'Don't try to escape,' Bere warned. The rope trailed behind him as he walked to the shallow water. He rinsed the blood off two turtle shells. Then he handed them to Maji. 'You know where the eggs are laid. Uncover them and fill the shells with the eggs. Push palm leaves in the openings so they won't fall out. And don't try to run.' He pulled the creeper rope up short and jerked it. 'You won't get far!'

The leopard man nodded. 'Go on. Do as he says. We'll dig a deeper grave for your father.'

The turtle eggs were easy to find. He followed the tracks above the high-water mark. In his arms he held the shells of the creatures that had made the tracks. Now the scutes were dry and the shells empty. He filled them with the same round white eggs that had been inside them before.

Three

When both jobs were done . . . one which required removing things from the earth, and the other which required returning something to the earth . . . the sun had already set.

He watched Bere dragging pieces of driftwood together. He yanked and ripped at the dry branches with movements too big for such a small job and tossed them into a pile. The other man crouched down and began steadily twirling a stick between the palms of his hands so that it rubbed against another stick. When a spark flickered, he blew gently until the flame came to life.

Maji lay on the sand just beyond the circle of their firelight. He watched the flecks of ash drift upwards as light as foam and planned his own escape. His stomach heaved as the smell of roasted turtle flesh filled his nostrils. He closed his eyes and pretended to sleep while he lay trying to catch the meaning of their words.

'We might as well kill him tonight. He's no use to us. He has no treasure. Let's kill him and move on in the morning.' It was the voice of the one called Bere.

'Yes . . . he has no treasure.'

'So?'

'Don't you see? He *is* the treasure!'

'What do you mean?'

'The boy has been to many places. He knows about trade. It'll please the Mambo.'

'And the Great Mambo has to be pleased!' Bere's words snapped back as impatiently as the sound of the sticks he had broken. After a while he spoke again. 'Why don't we sell a few turtle shells along the way? The Mambo wouldn't know.'

'Your words aren't wise! They could be whispered on the wind. The Mambo has spies.'

'We're far beyond the Kingdom now.'

'If he found out we'd traded freely, he'd have us killed.'

The one called Bere laughed harshly. 'If you were killed, the girl would be left behind. Unprotected! You would never risk that! The Mambo knows it. You've lost your spirit. You were once a free man. And now? Don't you want to be free once more?'

The wind shifted. Maji could not catch the other man's reply. Their voices were no more than a mumble now.

He must have slept. When he opened his eyes again, the sky was already light. He had missed the chance of escape. Somewhere in the night his fate had been decided. Now the leopard-cloaked man was already standing.

Maji narrowed his eyes against the rising sun as he watched the man tie the water-skins around his waist. Surely the one who carried the water-skins was the leader?

22

The man cut nine long palm-tree stakes. He stripped them of leaves and sharpened their ends with his dagger. He drove all nine deep into the sand at the water's edge. Then on to each sharp point he pushed the severed head of a turtle. In the early morning sunlight they cast long thin shadows that stretched towards Tamu's freshly dug grave.

A forest of terrible guardians.

'May their spirits return to the sea,' the man said.

Maji glanced quickly at him. It was the turtles' spirits he spoke of. But what of Tamu's spirit? How would Tamu's spirit ever find its way home to Kilwa?

The man turned. 'We must leave. It's half a day's journey to the mouth of the Sabi river. Our boat is tied there. We traded at Manekweni for beads. The others have gone ahead already.' He bent to load two of the egg-filled turtle shells on to his back and hung one across Maji's shoulder on a strip of hide.

Bere picked up some skin pouches then pulled impatiently at the rope tied to Maji's ankle. 'Come!'

The tide was low. Far out across the flat sea, a white line of surf hissed against the coral. He searched the sand for things from the dhow. But there was nothing. Not even a splinter of wood. Perhaps somewhere further down the coast, a three-sided sail lay floating on the sea. Torn. Floating like the wing of a giant sea bird.

The turtle shell thumped against his body as he walked. He listened to the gurgling of his stomach and the sound of his blood as it pushed through his body. The morning wore on. The rope chafed and pulled at

23

his ankle. The sand seemed to hold him back. Every time he slowed down, Bere walked harder. Once they stopped to dig for mussels in the sand. The leopard-cloaked man held out a cracked shell for Maji to eat. The flesh was gritty and tough but he forced himself to chew on it.

On and on they walked. The sun beat down fiercely. It hammered the sea into shining metal. They seemed to pass the same place again and again. In waves of shimmering heat the two men became four . . . then six . . . then eight. They came towards him and their faces swam around him separate from their bodies.

'He's worthless. Look at him staggering. He's thin. He's weak.'

The words floated around his head. We're wasting our time. He slows us down. Leave him to die. He's half dead already. The birds will finish him off. Or I'll finish him. One thrust is all that's needed!

Maji felt something sharp press against his neck.

'Keep your knife sheathed, Bere!' a voice commanded.

PART TWO
THE JOURNEY

Four

A sharp call woke Maji.

He eased himself up on to his elbows. He was no longer next to the sea but on a boat in the mouth of a wide river.

The leopard-cloaked man was standing with his back to him in the prow. His arms hung quietly at his sides and his head was tilted back as if waiting for something.

Then he whistled. A long drawn-out sound.

Maji saw a huge bird alight from the top of a dead tree. The leopard man flung a fish into the air. As it was about to land in the water, the bird swooped down. Massive wings beat the air. Images blurred. Claws stretched out and struck. Then the bird was back on the branch pulling at what it had caught.

The leopard man turned to Maji as if he had known he was watching. 'Hungwe, the fish eagle. The name means . . . great one passing through the sky . . . one who brings delight.' He held out a piece of papaya fruit. 'Here . . . eat! It'll give you strength. I had to carry you for the last part of the journey to the boat.'

Maji felt tired. So tired it seemed his bones were all in the wrong place. He sucked at the sweet orange papaya flesh and glanced around him.

The boat was made of rough pieces of wood held together with palm fibre and caulked with black resin. It was like the zambuco boats the traders used in the mangrove swamps. There was a small sail, or perhaps just an awning, made from strips of woven palm leaves. A piece of cloth lay over him. The creeper rope was still around his ankle.

Behind him was Bere. He sat uncloaked and was paddling hard. The strong muscles of his chest gleamed in the sunlight. Beyond Bere's shoulder, Maji caught sight of a patch of blue sea trapped between the dunes at the river mouth. For a moment he thought he saw the flash of a three-cornered sail riding on the waves. Could it be?

He had skimmed the surf with Tamu so often and glided into river mouths just like this one with the dhow's hull low in the water, heavy with a cargo of cotton. In the fading light they had sat in a still bend of river. The familiar stars of Kilwa gone. The new stars of an unknown place coming into the sky. The dhow's oil lamps swinging on the rigging, making patterns over the faces of the crew. Then they had slipped away again quietly before dawn on the out-going tide, laden with mangrove poles.

Now he watched the patch of sea slide away behind the dunes. It disappeared as silently as the shadow of a dhow's sail.

'Yes, look back! You'll never see the sea again!' Bere snarled.

The boat thrust forward against the current. Sunlight glittered and danced in small bright circles through the shade of the plaited palm sail. Maji's thoughts were like these specks of light. They darted around in his head. A shoal of silvery fish, never stopping long enough for him to catch one.

Where were they travelling? What would happen to him? Could he escape? Would he find his way back to Sofala? If he couldn't escape? What then? Would they kill him?

The leopard man stood balanced in the prow. He too had removed his skin cloak. Bands of gold and copper covered his neck. A small horn hung from his waistband next to his knife sheath. Thick veins snaked across the muscles of his chest and arms. Scars criss-crossed his forearms.

As he turned Maji caught his eye. 'By what name are you called?'

'Ingwe.'

'Leopard? The one with spots like the skin you wear?'

Ingwe looked at him with eyes as dark as water from a deep well.

Maji chewed at his lip. Then he asked the question that was making his tongue itch. 'Where are you taking me?'

'To the Kingdom of the Great Mambo.'

'Is there gold there?'

'Why do you ask?'

Maji shrugged. Tamu had spoken of a Kingdom of Gold that lay far from the sea. He drew scratches on parchment. Inky trails that were rivers. Small dots that were huge cities. Magic marks that only Tamu could change into real places with his stories. Now Maji heard the small plop sound of him plucking the stopper from the thick glass phial. He smelt the musty ink smell. Like the odour of a dark pool filled with weed. He heard the reed pen scratching against the parchment.

The voice of the leopard-cloaked man broke up the pictures in his head. 'This is the Sabi river. It takes us through mountains too difficult to cross on foot.'

'Is this Kingdom far?'

'So far that the sun will go down many, many times before we reach it. And the moon will be large, then shrink back, then grow large again.'

Maji pulled the cotton cloth closer around his shoulders. 'A whole moon's journey away from the sea?'

'Even more.'

'He questions too freely!' Bere's voice was harsh behind him.

How could it be that far? It was surely the Kingdom Tamu had spoken of. No person from Persia, or Cambaya, or Canton, or even Kilwa, had seen it. But many had whispered of it. On Tamu's map it had appeared as a tiny mark in the middle of a huge space. Empty and uncharted except for one large river. A river like a winding snake with its head in the sea and its tail stretching far into an unknown land where the sun went down.

Maji chewed even harder on his lip until his eyes smarted. The idea of a Kingdom that lay so very far from the sea frightened him even more than these men!

The sun dipped behind the mangrove trees. Dark reflections of roots and twisted branches reached out like the pincers of a crab as the boat slid past. But beneath the boat he sensed the force of the water. The pull of the downstream current was strong. Its strength gave him courage. It would help him escape.

When the light faded, they pulled over to the bank. Bere spiked a fish. He held it towards Maji on the point of his spear. 'A catfish! See! Whiskers like a cat!' On the little finger of Bere's right hand he saw the flash of silver and the deep colours of cornelian and lapis lazuli.

The men ate strips of raw fish in silence. He swallowed just enough to give him strength for the long swim he needed to make that night. The sun's heat was still trapped in the wood of the boat. Sounds of frogs, mosquitoes and grunting sea-cows drifted across the water. Then the moon rose large and full over the tangled mangroves.

When had he last seen it rising full? Was it over the evening market in Kilwa? Tables laden with fish. Plucked birds. Coconuts with sweet, milky juice. Crunchy nut clinging to the hard shells. Baskets of limes and betel leaves for traders to chew on. Globs of betel-stained spit glistening like red rubies in the alleyways. A scent of oranges. Strong herbs. A sweet smell of butter and honey. Trees hung with beehives woven from palm leaves. The warm evening air still humming with bees.

He longed for the smell and taste of these things. When the men were sleeping he would cut the rope on his ankle. He would swim downstream and escape back to Kilwa.

'Keep watch for crocodiles!'

Bere spoke so suddenly, Maji jumped. He snatched his hand back from the water. Could Bere have read his thoughts?

'Tonight the moon will light their eyes like coals.'

And later, Maji saw the red eyes sprinkled across the river like jewels in a brilliant ruby necklace. Bere was right. Escape was impossible. With so many crocodiles, he would never be able to swim back to the coast.

Five

The next day as they paddled, Maji smelt wood-smoke. Suddenly there was a splashing sound as if a herd of sea-cows had been disturbed. A group of women and children scrambled up the bank. The children were naked and the women wore leather aprons. Their necks and arms were stiff with strands of shell beads and shiny cowries. Their hair was coated with thick red mud. They held loosely woven fishing baskets that tapered to narrow bottoms.

'Greetings, mothers of children!' Ingwe called out. 'Tonight we honour your fire.'

Around the next bend, five young girls stood with pounding sticks, singing as each blow fell into a hollowed-out tree stump. The air was smoky. And the black burnt ground tufted with bright-green new grass. Ingwe tied their boat to a tree alongside three long dugout canoes that were pulled up on to the bank. Children rushed into the river to help. They stared at Maji and giggled. Then they followed in a line behind Ingwe and Bere, and every now and again one of them reached out to touch Maji's arm.

A group of men sat in the shade of some tall ilala palms. Ingwe and Bere exchanged greetings with them and spoke in a quick language Maji couldn't follow. The men sat cross-legged, their eyes fixed on him, the lobes of their ears stretched with the weight of heavy shell earrings.

That evening as they sat around the fire telling stories and eating fish with millet cakes, Maji planned another escape. This time it would be easier. He wouldn't have to swim. He'd steal a dugout canoe and paddle downstream. He would reach the coast before dawn.

But later when the fire died down and the sky was drowned in moonlight, Bere's hands were brisk. He tied Maji's wrists behind his back and bound his feet together as well.

'You're still held to my waist! Don't try to escape!' Then he disappeared through the opening of a hut.

Maji knew he couldn't miss a third chance. He needed to free his hands and feet and cut the ankle rope. A sharp stone would do. But there were no stones lying about. If he could reach the cluster of ilala palms, rubbing against the bark would break the rope. But when he tried to ease his way across the earth towards the palms, the rope was not quite long enough.

Panic rose in him. In this village of fish-eaters, tied to Bere, he felt separate and apart. More alone than ever before. Now he would never escape. His head was full of scared thoughts. He was truly afraid. Afraid of the dark shadows that clustered below the palms. Afraid of the whispering in the leaves. Afraid to be so far from the sea. Afraid of the Kingdom that lay ahead.

He curled up on his side against the earth and the moonlight covered him like a skin.

When he woke, a faint light already streaked the sky. The stars had faded. A crested crane flew overhead. A new day was breaking. He had survived the night. When some village men walked past, he tried to signal that he wanted to be untied. But they climbed into their dugouts and slipped between the mangroves. Later he heard the *thunk thunk* of blades against the mangrove poles. They could have cut the ropes so easily.

When it was time to leave, Bere untied his hands and feet. Some children poled alongside their boat in dugout canoes. They laughed and shouted as they tried to keep up. Then the gap between the boats widened. They slackened off and stood waving.

How could they be so happy?

Six

After the sun had risen three times at their backs, they reached a place where the river broke into narrow passages between reed islands. Now they cut strong pieces of cane and poled with them where the water was shallow.

The reeds grew so tall that the plumes met overhead like the roof of a mosque. In the quietness Maji listened to the sound of the poles as they sucked away from the mud. Every time they struck down, they were a boat's length further from the sea.

Suddenly three slender dugouts slid out from a narrow stream between the reeds. They were poled by three silent men. The boats hung low in the water. Each boat held a huge dead crocodile sprawled along its length. Massive tails and legs hung over the sides, dragging in the water. Huge jaws gaped open, showing rows of yellowed teeth.

Then just as silently as they had appeared, they slipped between the reeds and disappeared without a gap showing which waterway they had taken.

'Who are they?' Maji whispered.

'Crocodile hunters. They kill for the skins.'

That night they sat on the boat in a temple of reeds. The air was so quiet and hot it was impossible to sleep. A single clap of thunder shattered the silence. Maji heard the rain and wind approaching from a distance. It rustled through the reeds until a deafening roar surrounded the boat. In sudden brilliant flashes the plumes became an army of clashing spears. Then just as suddenly, the storm passed and it was silent again.

The next morning the boat was wrapped in steamy mist and broken reed.

An arrow came from nowhere.

As silent as a bird, it sliced the air. As swift as a cormorant diving for fish, it plunged into the water next to them.

'The crocodile hunters!' Ingwe whispered.

A second arrow stung deep into Maji's thigh. Within seconds his leg was burning as if a thousand wasps had stung him.

'Quick! Press your groin!' Ingwe hissed. 'Their arrowheads are dipped in poison. Don't let it spread.' He thrust a stick between Maji's teeth. 'Bite on this! Forget everything else!'

There was a sudden sharp pain. Maji peered down at the slim shaft still wedged in his flesh. Ingwe had cut two clean slashes on either side of it.

'Don't look!' Ingwe commanded as he grasped the shaft.

The pain made sounds in Maji's head. He bit hard into the wood.

When the arrowhead came out, bits of flesh were stuck to it. He watched the blood well up and start to flow in the wound. Ingwe sucked at it and spat. Sucked and spat. Then he reached for the small horn tied to his waistband. He pressed the hollow end over the wound, sucked hard at a small hole in the tip, then clamped the hole closed with his thumb.

'It'll draw the poison.'

Maji felt the pressure of the horn against his skin. 'What is the poison?'

'Venom from snakes mixed with poisonous bulbs. Be hopeful it's not venom from a puff-adder.'

'What if it is?'

Ingwe shrugged.

Bere's eyes were narrow. 'No one recovers from a puff-adder. The crocodile hunters marked you!'

'Hold your tongue, Bere! Pole to the bank! Maji, keep the horn in place with your thumb held tightly over the hole.'

The boat bumped ground.

'Wait here!' Ingwe slipped into the undergrowth and disappeared as silently as the crocodile hunters.

Now he sat alone in the boat with Bere staring at him. He would not let him think he was scared. The branches made shadow patterns across Bere's face. A heavy scar ran across his left cheek. A small piece was nicked out of one ear. It seemed he had fought many battles.

Bere removed his knife from its carved wooden sheath. The same knife he had used to carve the flesh of the turtles from their shells. He began to toss it from hand to hand.

It was a sturdy knife. Made for his hand. With a handle of bone. Bound with brass and copper wire. Riveted with two metal pins. It was a knife that had been weighted, honed and fashioned on a quiet day when hands had not hurried over the work. Pointed enough to whittle the finest breastbone. Sharp enough to hack through the sturdiest thighbone. It was a knife for hacking. Thrusting. Trimming. Cutting. Skinning. Killing.

All of these things.

Bere stroked his thumb delicately back and forth across the blade as if to test it. In the shadow, the lapis lazuli on his little finger was as dark as a deep pool and the cornelian glowed red as blood.

The forest had swallowed Ingwe. Maji listened to the silence. All around he felt the presence of the crocodile hunters. Their eyes watching behind damp leaves. Their poisoned arrows ready. Waiting. Just as Bere seemed to be waiting.

He had only the horn. Bere had a knife. Sharp and fine.

A twig snapped. Maji jumped. Suddenly the tree above was alive with noise. A troop of tiny grey monkeys squabbled and jumped and crashed along the branches over their heads.

Bere jeered. 'They're only tsoko. Are you frightened of tsoko?'

Then Maji saw it! He stood up so suddenly, the boat nearly overturned. The thing swivelled slowly on a creeper and swayed and bounced in the shadows as the monkeys ran along the branch that it hung from. Flies rose in clouds, then settled again in thick black clusters, seething and jostling for more. A thick swollen tongue hung from the gaping mouth. The eyes were each pierced by an arrow.

It was only the head. Yet hanging by a creeper with feathered arrows dangling from its eyes, it seemed more frightening than any live crocodile.

Bere laughed. 'It's the hunters. To show their power. But I warn you, mine is greater.'

Then Ingwe was suddenly next to them. He held an armful of leaves.

Maji pointed to the crocodile head.

Ingwe shrugged. 'It's to scare us. To warn us away from their territory. The arrow was a warning as well.' He took the horn away. 'You're lucky. The poison is not from a puff-adder.'

'How do you know?'

'A puff-adder's venom would have turned the wound white already.' He squeezed juice from a waxy leaf into the wound and crushed leaves into a thick pad, which he bound in place with creepers. 'This will draw the poison.'

Seven

He lies burning.

Threads of darkness weave through his head.

As the threads grow, they trap his thoughts.

Somewhere a fish eagle keens. High-pitched. Lonely.

He needs to follow the call.

In Kilwa the sea shines like a thousand beads.

At high tide it laps the entrance to the Husuni Kubwa Palace where the dhows tie up.

With gold and copper coins the merchants trade for flasks of perfume. Incense. Resin. Thick blue glass from Persia. Gold-threaded cloth. Bracelets made of silver. Pearls as big as dove's eggs. Turquoise and cornelian.

He runs wild between the traders. Sniffing the scents. Touching the silks and the silver. Skidding over the rotten fruit and betel spit in the alleyways.

Always there is Tamu and the cool house to return to. The latticed courtyard and the pomegranate tree laden with red fruit. The smell of oranges. Figs. Parchment. Bottles of murky ink. And the sweet aroma of fish cooked in lime juice and coconut milk flavoured with tamarind.

He sees Tamu's face criss-crossed with lines. So many, there is no space to lay a finger between them. Tamu's eyes are screwed up against the glare of the sun. Rough stubble marks his top lip. Long thin fingers wind his head-cloth. He tucks in the ends in one quick movement that's too fast to follow. Something Maji can never do quite well enough.

It needs one swift movement. Lower, Maji! Lower! Tamu laughs. It's to keep you cool. To shade you from the sun!

But he is hot. A hot fever burns him.

The poison threads trap his thoughts.

He is not in Kilwa. He is on a lonely shore.

He lies alongside Tamu. Damp sand covers his face. Small creatures pick the soft parts of his body clean. His bones lie with Tamu's bones. Turtles make paths over them in the moonlight. The wind lays bare their bones. In the hot sun the bones whiten and shift apart.

But no matter. Their spirits are together. Flying free over the water.

Yet in the heat of the fever, he knows he will die far from where Tamu lies. Far from the sea.

When he dies how will his spirit know where to find Tamu's spirit?

Something covers his eyes. He smells herbs. He hears voices.

'Hold his leg down. We must keep the leaves fresh. Pack them tightly.'

'He has a mark on his leg. Look! On the inside of his thigh.'

'What of it? He's not the first to be born with a mark.'

'But not in the shape of a strange creature. I tell you, it's the mark of evil!'

It's the mark of something special . . . Maji wants to shout. Something still to be revealed. Tamu has told him. But the poison blocks his mouth. His head is matted with spider webs. Only his ears are open.

'The mark shows he's touched by an evil spirit. Leave him to die!'

'What if it's the mark of a good spirit?'

Maji smiles. Yes . . . Ingwe understands.

Later he feels a rocking movement. He is lying on the floor of a boat. The sunlight dances red through a lattice of leaves that cover him. There is sweat running down a man's back.

Another time it is night. Through the mesh of leaves he sees a moon. It's no longer full but sharp and thin. Curved like a blade.

Then there is the hissing sound of water. Rocks reach up and catch at the base of the boat. He knows the sound. The rocks snap as sharply as teeth of coral at the dhow. But this is not the dhow. He is with Ingwe and Bere. They are fighting a current in a narrow gorge.

Suddenly, Maji finds the strength to wrench himself awake.

They swing around. Go plunging back downstream again. Sweeping sideways. Thrust on by the rapids. Hurtling over rocks that seem to want to rip them apart. The boat shudders and twists like a piece of wrung cloth.

He strains to balance. He grabs at overhanging branches to keep the boat from overturning. There is no time to think, only to grip tight and throw his weight as they swirl through the churning water and are sucked down in the undertow. Then the boat is thrown up against a tree.

Maji grabs a branch and hangs on. Water hisses past on either side. Ingwe is shouting. The water drowns his voice. Someone holds on to his ankles. He feels his arms being wrenched from their sockets. He clings desperately. Bere and Ingwe manage to grab the branch as well. Then they ease sideways, clutching hand-over-hand along the branch until they have pulled the boat with the strength of their legs out of the swirl of the current.

'Ahee-yah!' Ingwe shook his head. 'The Kapsuku rapids are fierce this year. Fierce enough to wake Maji from his poison-sleep.'

'He has brought too many troubles. An evil spirit is loose with him here!'

'There is no evil spirit, Bere. The rapids are fierce because the water is low. The rocks are too close to the surface.'

'We're too heavy with him in the boat,' Bere snapped.

'Without his help, we might have lost the boat and the turtle shells and the Manekweni beads with it. We must carry the boat around the Kapsuku cliffs. We'll take the path of the elephant,' Ingwe said, pointing to one of the crevices, 'and walk through the musimbiti trees.'

Eight

That night under the branches of a huge musimbiti, the fire sucked heavy moths into the circle of light. Maji studied Ingwe. Why was this man protecting him? Where were they taking him? Questions flew about in his head, as troubled as the moths, singeing their wings.

'Is the Kingdom still far?' he asked.

'What is distance? Ask rather . . . are we safe? You slept while the leaf medicine did its work. Many suns have set since we met the crocodile hunters.'

Maji looked down at his leg. It was still bound but not throbbing. Yes, Ingwe had done a good job. He looked back at him. 'How did your people come to live in a kingdom that is so far?'

Bere snorted. 'How did fish first swim in the sea?'

'But is it large?'

'Larger than any you will ever see.'

'I've seen the Palace of Husuni Kubwa.'

Bere peered at Maji through the smoke and laughed. 'That is nothing. The Kingdom of Dzimba Dzemabwe covers the earth like a cloud that blocks the whole sky.'

'How can one man rule a kingdom so large?'

'With gold. And with fire.'

Maji glanced from one to the other. Gold was easy to understand. It was something of trade. But fire? Was the Mambo a fire-god that spurted fire from his mouth? A dragon creature with flaming nostrils? He had seen such a creature painted in blue on eating-bowls from Canton.

'How does he come by the gold?'

Ingwe poked a stick into the fire. Sparks flew into the air and mingled with the moths. 'In the time of long ago, it was found in river sand. People were greedy. They knew they could trade with it. Gold can enter a man's heart like blood, until without it he's nothing. Why else would anyone want to dig into the earth like a warthog snuffling and burrowing into a termite mound?'

The firelight seemed to draw words from Ingwe.

'Soon the gold in the sand disappeared, but they found more. Not in sand, this time, but deep under the earth. At the place of the Great Rock they dig tunnels to bring it out. They grind the rock with gold in it. Then they heat the rock-dust over a fire until it turns to water that is not water but gold . . .'

'Tchh!' Bere clicked his tongue. 'You make the story too long! It's enough to know the people of the Great Rock take the gold to the coast for trade. They have to pass through the Kingdom. The Great Mambo demands some of it.'

'Some?'

'Not just some. More than half!'

'But why? If they have done all the work?'

Bere grinned. 'For a safe passage through the Kingdom!'

'What if they don't give him the gold?'

Bere made a single slicing motion across his throat.

Maji stared back at Bere. The firelight made a terrifying mask of his face. A shiver ran through Maji. He looked across at Ingwe. Surely he would say something to suggest Bere's gesture was foolishness? But Ingwe remained silent as he stared into the flames.

Praise Allah! What were the words he should be praying? There was no one to protect him now. Not even Ingwe could protect him from a ruler who killed so ruthlessly.

In the shadows at his back, he heard strange rustlings. As if something was prowling. He listened for a soft tread. But he was too scared to look over his shoulder. Too scared to ask about the fire-power. Too scared to even think. He had escaped the poison of the arrow. But now? What lay ahead?

Under the branches of the musimbiti tree the shadows pressed down heavily. His heart beat high up in his throat. He felt unable to breathe. His fate was decided. He was being taken to a kingdom with a ruler who was fiercer and more terrifying than any crocodile. They had travelled too far for him *ever* to escape now.

He felt the darkness of the night settle on him.

Nine

For the next few days Maji thought about the narrow trickle of river shimmering in the sunlight behind him. He was a spider. The river was his thread. Just as the dhow's wake had tied him to Kilwa, now this thin thread of water tied him to the sea and Tamu. And like a spider returning to his web, he would have to crawl back along the thread if he ever wanted to return.

Eventually the river withered to nothing. All that was left were muddy pools pitted with animal tracks. The boat was no longer of use. They unloaded it and Ingwe stuck two strong forked branches into the ground some distance from the riverbed. They left it hanging between its resting posts like a man asleep in a hammock.

'Others might have use for it, if they come this way,' Ingwe said.

Then they followed the riverbed. Finally even the muddy pools dried up, leaving only a sandy track between thorn trees. Maji tried to visualize water seeping and moving through the dry sand under his feet. Yet he could not imagine even the smallest underground stream.

Nothing connected him to the sea any longer. He was never going back. He wrenched a branch from a tree. With a sharp stone he slashed a white gash into the bark. It marked the first day that separated him from his other life. His life without the sea!

Every day they rose early and walked hard. The stony ground hardened Maji's heels as they travelled further and further into this strange country. Long sharp spikes grew from leafless trees. Bark curled and cracked like a lizard's skin. Huge seedpods rattled against each other in the dry wind. Locusts' wings clicked.

And the grass whispered . . . the sea is too far . . . the sea is too far!

He looked at the ground. He studied the trees. He watched the sky. He tried to compare it with places he'd travelled to before.

Yet everything was different. The sky held no blue. The earth no richness. The sun had sucked up every colour. The silent glimmering land with its heat-shimmer of water when there was none, confused him.

He watched Ingwe and Bere with slow sidelong glances. They dug out fleshy roots where he thought nothing grew. They gathered sweet-tasting milkberries from scrawny bushes. They found sap under shrivelled bark and juice inside strange-looking fruit. They took their direction from the sun and stars and the way in which the termite mounds sloped. They climbed trees to outwit buffalo. They stood still to deceive elephant. Where he saw only rocks, they saw buck. When he heard only wind, they heard lion calling.

He watched and listened to Ingwe whisper, 'May your spirit give strength to our spirits,' every time he sliced through the thick pulsing vein in the neck of anything he speared. Then they roasted the flesh on sticks over a fire. As he ate, Maji felt the strength of the animal enter his own body.

At night they slept on hard ground with rocks as their headrests, protected by the spirits of the huge, strangely-shaped trees, which seemed to grow upside down with their roots in the air.

The sun rose many times at their back and the marks on his stick grew too many to be counted.

Sometimes he caught Ingwe looking at Bere with hard, narrow eyes that told nothing. No words were spoken. But there was fire between them. A fire that burned not with heat but with ice. The air seemed to crackle between them.

And then . . . ? And then he sensed a change.

Now against the vastness of the country, Ingwe and Bere seemed to shrink.

They took only small sips from the water-skins that had been filled at the last pools. They set off earlier each morning while the sky was dark and the stars still bright. They walked only until the sun rose. When the sun shot its first spears over the horizon and their shadows were still long and thin, they stopped to rest. Through the heat of the day they sat in the net-like shadows of scrawny trees watching falcons hawk the dry air. They stared across a land shimmering through heat waves like the ocean, careful of the curve-tailed scorpion lurking under stones and the coiled cobra resting in crevices.

Now with no water left in the water-skins, they turned to the turtle eggs. They punctured the tough leathery shells. When Ingwe held one out to him, Maji cupped the egg close to his mouth and whispered, 'May your spirit give strength to my spirit.' Then he sipped the thick, yolky mixture.

The hot air sucked at him until he felt as sapless as the pale grass and as brittle as the twigs that snapped between his fingers. Against the vastness of the country he too had shrunk to nothing.

Perhaps they would never reach the Kingdom.

Ten

And then . . . ? Then it happened.

He found the stick.

It seemed quite an ordinary stick. He was collecting firewood when he saw the sapling between the crisp-gold mopani trees. It was pliant and sappy with green tasty buds. He cut it down. The soft bark was covered with fine hairs.

Suddenly as he held it, the branch twitched in his hands. He grasped the two prongs firmly, one in each hand. The main branch jerked again. Then flipped over in a complete circle. Yet the stick looked ordinary enough. He stuck it in a girdle he'd made of plaited bark, along with his other day-marking stick.

That night while he lay watching the unfamiliar star-patterns slip silently across the sky, a strange shriek stabbed the darkness. He waited, holding his breath. Then it came again, rising higher and higher, a long hollow drawn-out *whoop . . . whoop . . . whoop . . .* that ended with frightening laughter.

He lay stiff waiting for the sound to stop. Hardly daring to breathe. What spirit had the stick called?

The next morning, Bere eyed him. 'Why do you carry a green stick in your waistband?'

'It's . . .' he bit his lip trying to think of something to say. 'It's . . . for holding down snakes when I'm collecting wood.'

'Liar!' Bere snatched the stick and held it up in front of Maji's face. 'An important stick, it seems! Why?'

'Stop tormenting him!' Ingwe grabbed it and tossed it back to Maji.

When he was far from where they sat, he took the stick in his hands again. It twisted as sharply as a cobra. He threw it down.

'The stick has spoken. Pick it up!' It was Bere's voice behind him. 'How long have you had the power?'

Maji stared at him. 'What power?'

'The power of the stick. How long has it been yours?'

Maji shook his head. 'I have no power.'

'Speak the truth!' Bere grabbed his shoulder. 'You've found water. Where is it?'

'There is none!'

'The stick speaks of water under the earth. You have the gift of a water diviner!' Bere paced backwards and forwards. 'Stand here!' He pushed Maji to where he was pointing.

There was nothing on the ground except dust.

'Hold the stick as before.'

Maji's hands were stiff. If Bere wanted the stick to move, he would have to turn it himself. But suddenly the stick spun so sharply that Maji jumped as well.

'Mark the spot!' Bere ordered. He shoved a stone towards him. 'Now turn around. Walk this way.'

Again the stick swung as if it wanted to twist out of his hands. Bere marked the place with another stone. Then pushed him in a new direction. Each time Maji walked, the stick came alive. Eventually there were five stones marking out a circle.

'The spirit will be angry,' Maji said, looking over his shoulder.

'What spirit?'

'The one the stick called last night.'

'There was no spirit.'

'There was! It shrieked and laughed . . .'

'Fool! That was Bere. The hyena. The one I'm named for. Have you never heard a hyena's call? Now dig there!'

He didn't have to dig. He stood with his hands loosely at his sides and he knew . . . he knew without being able to say why or how . . . there was water beneath his feet. He felt it under his soles. He felt it like a stream pulling at his body. Drawing him towards it.

'Dig!' Bere ordered.

Dribbles of water gathered in hollows as he worked. It seeped up clear before mingling with the mud. Bere pushed him aside, dipped his hands into it and licked the drops from his fingers. Then he shouted for Ingwe.

Maji remained silent. His arms tingled. His body listened. The stick had found water. Water had been calling him all this time from deep under the hard dry ground from where it ran in streams . . . just like blood through his own flesh. Now he felt it under his soles pushing its way through the ground deep below him. Travelling back to the sea.

He knelt down and put his ear to the ground. Surely something he felt so strongly, he would hear also?

'The mark on your leg is the sign,' Ingwe said as he stood beside him. 'It's a water sign.'

'How do you know?'

Ingwe glanced at him strangely. 'I've lived with water people.'

Maji squatted down to examine the mark more closely. The more he looked, the more certain it seemed. The shape was a turtle. Tamu had been right. He thought of Tamu's words. In the language of KiSwahili, Maji means . . . water. But with this sign, it means . . . Spirit Water.

Now the water-skins were full again.

They walked with swinging arms and long strides. Blue-faced hanga birds and brown-speckled hwari birds flew up startled from the grass. The land changed. Huge towering boulders balanced on top of one another, as if waiting to topple down on anyone walking below. Ingwe and Bere's mouths were full of names now.

'The rock is Rushumbi.'

'See the dry riverbeds of the Mazuli and Meziro rivers.'

'That pointed tooth is Arowi. See how it dances in the heat mist of the Moshagashi valley.'

'Look! The Motelekwe has stopped flowing. There are only trapped pools.'

'Yes . . .' Ingwe nodded. 'The river that suckles the Kingdom is drying up!'

They splashed in the pools with dragonflies and tiny brilliant kingfishers hovering around their faces. Then the path became steep and winding. It passed through cliffs full of caves and dark crevices. Further along, Maji found a feather at his feet.

'Pick it up!' Bere commanded.

Maji smoothed the dark spars that had parted from one another.

'It's a message for you.'

'What?'

'An omen. Sent from the heavens.'

The black feather glinted with a coppery sheen in the sunlight. Its shaft was strong and white. What was the omen?

'It's from the Chapungu eagle.' Bere's eyes challenged Ingwe's. 'One that is greater than Hungwe!'

Now beneath their feet the land plunged into a long valley. They walked in a straight line towards the sun.

'Look there,' Bere pointed, 'through the gap in the Beroma rocks. Do you see the Mambo's Houses of Stone?'

Maji shaded his eyes. He stared towards the setting sun at the place where the rocks met the sky. At first it seemed no more than a pile of huge, round boulders. They lay like massive dogs basking in the last warmth of the sun. Then he saw the walls of stone. They wound over and between the rocks and curved along the edge of the steep ridge. Along the walls were stone turrets and thin shafts of stones. They pointed like fingers into the red sky.

'That is the Kingdom of Dzimba Dzemabwe!'

As they got closer Maji stopped and looked down. In the valley below, a stone city lay behind a haze of purple wood-smoke. From its centre rose a massive tower surrounded by more stone walls. Row upon row of small mud buildings covered the entire valley from one ridge to the other. They rose in terraces up the side of the nearest ridge. Between the buildings, he could see people moving like termites in a nest. The air was heavy with the smell of wood-fire, dust and dung. There was a steady drumming sound as if heavy raindrops were falling on large leaves, yet it wasn't raining.

The Kingdom was truly larger than anything he had ever seen.

Maji felt his bones freeze even though the evening was still warm.

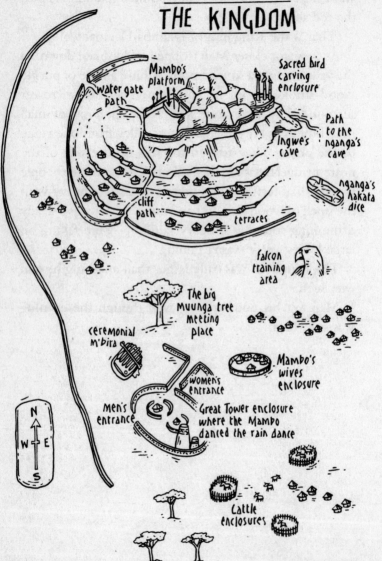

THE KINGDOM

water gate path

Mambo's platform

Sacred bird carving enclosure

Ingwe's cave

Path to the nganga's cave

nganga's hakata dice

cliff path

terraces

falcon training area

The big Muunga tree meeting place

ceremonial m'bira

women's entrance

Mambo's wives enclosure

Men's entrance

Great Tower enclosure where the Mambo danced the rain dance

N
W   E
S

Cattle enclosures

PART THREE
THE KINGDOM

Eleven

'They say you have magic powers with a stick!'

Hmm! Maji looked at the boy who had spoken. How did he know about the stick already? Ingwe had only a moment ago left him here with these boys. He stood in the shadows silently studying their faces in the firelight as they crouched around a large clay cooking pot. They had skins tied around their waists and dust in their hair and sat digging into the pot as if they'd never seen food before.

'Well? Is it true?' the same boy asked between mouthfuls of food.

A second boy sat back on his haunches and caught Maji's eyes. He shrugged a loose careless shrug so that his long thin arms dangled. 'Here, news travels quicker than drumbeats. It's our way. We're cattle herders. We look out and we watch . . .'

The first boy interrupted. 'Shut your mouth, Jee!' Then he glanced back at Maji. 'How will you find water if there *is* no water?'

The boy called Jee ignored the first boy. 'How does a stick find water?'

'Jee, have you nothing in your head? It's not the stick that finds the water. It's him. They say he has power in him to find water.'

Maji looked hard at this boy who seemed to have so many answers. He spoke as if he'd lived a long time. What did he know of finding water?

The boy with the thin arms called Jee stood up. 'We've forgotten how we were taught to greet strangers. We see you. If you are well, then we are well. We're glad that you have honoured our fire.' He gestured towards the pot. 'Please sit and eat with us. My name is Jee. And my friend who is so fast to tell how clever he is, is Mufudzi.'

The one called Mufudzi scowled at them. But before Maji could say anything, both he and Jee had their hands back in the pot.

'I am Maji,' he said to the back of their heads.

Jee stopped and looked up for a moment. He licked a thick wad of millet porridge off his thumb and smiled. 'We know!'

Was there anything they didn't know?

'Your sleeping mat is on the ground!' Mufudzi said, frowning at him.

So . . . ? Maji chewed his lip and stopped himself from asking . . . where else should a sleeping mat be?

'That's my place where you have put it!'

Jee waved his arms loosely. 'Mufudzi likes to sleep near the entrance of the hut. You should store it in the roof-poles so the ishwa ants don't make nests under it.'

Maji kept silent. At least he could imagine what ishwa ants were. In KiSwahili, 'ishiwa na' meant to have none left. So ishwa ants would chew up his sleeping mat. He would have nothing left.

Mufudzi stopped eating for a moment and gave him a hard look. 'Can you fight with your stick?'

He shrugged. 'I don't know. I haven't tried.'

'You come from a strange place if you can't stick fight!' Mufudzi went back to digging in the pot. When it was empty, he stood up and wiped his hands against his dusty thighs. He looked at Maji through half closed eyes. 'Shall we stick fight now? Let's test your stick!'

Jee stood up. 'Maji's stick is for finding water, not for fighting.'

Maji glanced at him. Why was this boy so concerned?

Then Jee stretched and yawned. 'In any case now's not the time for stick fighting.'

'Why not?' Mufudzi snapped.

'Tomorrow we have far to go. The cattle must be taken to new pastures. We have to leave early. Now we must sleep.'

'Since when do you make the decisions?' Mufudzi challenged. Then he shrugged carelessly as if it were not worth discussing. 'Very well. There's plenty of time for stick fighting.' He clicked his fingers and held out his hand. One of the younger herders pulled a piece of thatching grass from the roof of the hut and handed it to him Mufudzi squatted down and began drawing plans in the dust for where they should take the cattle the next day.

Maji's eyes followed the boy called Jee. He wanted to say something to him, but Jee was already disappearing into the hut. He could see him unrolling his mat on the ground.

When the others had all arranged their mats, Maji found an empty space as far away from Mufudzi as possible.

In the darkness he lay stiff, listening to the strange noises of the Kingdom. A baby crying. Music twanging. Voices murmuring. And over it all the sound of the drums throbbing like a heartbeat.

It was hard to sort out all the things that had happened to him since he entered the Kingdom. Children running up out of the shadows, skipping and shouting around them. Dogs barking and sniffing at their heels. Voices calling out greetings. Bere disappearing. Ingwe calling a girl forward from an enclosure.

He had slid his eyes to the ground. In Kilwa it was forbidden to look at a girl. In Kilwa girls remained inside latticed courtyards. He had seen the blue stripe around the bottom of her wrap. Her hands were small as she offered him some water in a gourd. Then she held out a clay serving dish of steaming relish that filled the air with strange herby flavours. It was sharp and different to anything he had ever tasted before. Then Ingwe handed him a sleeping mat and led him here to the herders' enclosure.

Now he was with these strange boys who eyed him suspiciously and who seemed to know everything. And beyond the firelight was nothing but a land that sent shivers through him.

As he lay listening, a hyena started its long drawn-out

whoop . . . whoop . . . whoop . . . that ended with a hideous cackle. The sound echoed and repeated itself against the rocks. Where was Bere now? Later in his dreams he sensed the dark shape of a hyena standing over him. He felt the hot stink of its breath against his face.

Twelve

He woke confused the next morning. The sharp smell of reed, bitter wood-smoke and dust scratched his throat. Next to his face a small, almost transparent gecko resettled itself on the mud wall.

Then it came to him. He had slept inside the herders' hut. From the small strip of sunlight that fell through the door, he sensed the sun was already high overhead. The herders must have long been gone. Their mats were rolled up in the roof-poles above his head and the sand was covered with their footprints. Or could the pads of a hyena not have made some? He shivered and felt for his water-stick. It was still safely in his girdle.

He heard the sound of a horn and loud drumming. Now he could hear people hurrying. A shadow fell across the sunlight as Ingwe stepped into the hut. He was wearing a woven cloth with a length of it thrown over his shoulder. There were red slashes across his right forearm, as if he had wrestled with a wild animal.

'You have slept long. The horn is calling us. The Mambo will ask the ancestral spirits for rain. Here, tie this around your waist.' He handed Maji a piece of cloth.

Nothing had prepared Maji for the sight of the huge crowd gathered at the meeting place under a spreading thorn tree. Unlike Ingwe most of them were dressed in skins. They pushed between the people until they reached a stone wall, which rose like a sheer cliff. They passed through a narrow opening and entered an enclosure. To their right was the stone tower that Maji had seen the night before. A band of purple stones like crocodile teeth ran around its upper part. A smaller tower stood next to it. Men were tapping skin drums that stood nearly as tall as the men themselves.

A high-pitched wailing rose above the drumming.

Everyone fell silent as a long line of women appeared. They held on to each other's waists. Small puffs of dust rose as they tapped each foot three times before stepping forward. In the dusty light, their heavy bands of gold bracelets and neckbands glinted like small suns as they chanted and circled the inside of the enclosure.

'Are they slaves?' Maji whispered.

'The Mambo's wives.'

'So many?'

A man was plucking at thin metal strips wired over a hollow gourd.

Ingwe caught Maji's glance. 'The m'bira player. He calls the spirits of the Mambo's ancestors.'

'Why?' A shiver ran through Maji. He felt for the water-stick in his girdle. Would its power be enough to help him face the spirits of the Mambo's ancestors?

'The spirits live in the rocks close to the sky.' Ingwe pointed at the thin shafts of stone that looked like daggers sticking out from the tops of the walls. 'See . . . the stones represent the spirits. They're the Horns of the Mambo. The spirits are being called today to ask for rain. The Mambo dances a special dance to ask them to plead before the Great God Mwari.'

The m'bira music grew louder. People beat iron gongs and rattled seeds in dry gourds. They circled the walls and shouted, 'Great Mambo of the Sun and Moon! Lord of the Land! Lord of the Rivers! Conqueror of Enemies! Great Lion! Great Crocodile!'

'Who are they?' Maji whispered.

'Praise-singers.'

Suddenly, like a shaft of strong sunlight, a gold figure appeared on a stone platform. He stretched his arms towards the last rays of the sun. The light glinted on the layer of gold sheeting that covered his body. A mask of golden hair sprouted from his face like the mane of a fierce lion. He seemed entirely made of gold.

'Is he the Mambo?' He chewed his lip. Was this the fire creature?

'It could be the Mambo. Or the Spirit of the Rain. Or the Spirit of the Great Lion.' Bere's voice spoke in riddles behind him.

The golden figure thrust back his head. His shoulders hunched forward and his arms stretched out. He crouched on the platform. Half man. Half lion. Then he began to dance. Slowly at first. Then faster. His head flicked. His body jerked. His feet beat stiffly. His gaze never left the enclosure down below.

Maji felt as if he could not tear his eyes away.

The music grew faster and faster. The lion-man became a fireball of golden light spinning around the edge of the stone platform in the last shafts of the setting sun. Drums, rattles, gongs, m'biras and chanting echoed around the walls. There was no space for any other sound in Maji's head.

In the purple light people were dancing their own spirit dance. Bracelets and neckbands gleamed. Through swirls of cloth, masked faces jumped forward.

Maji felt dizzier and dizzier. Who was real? Who was spirit?

Arms beckoned him. Hands grabbed at him. His feet were swept off the ground. Sometimes he stumbled. Then he was tugged into a narrow stone passage. A torch flared in a stone niche above him. He saw a girl. She was wearing a cloth with a blue stripe around the edge. Was it the girl who had brought him water? A thin film of sweat reflected on her face. She danced with her arms moving like the wings of a small bird and her hands were like butterflies.

A shadow fell between them. It was Ingwe. He spoke sharply to the girl. She disappeared down a passageway.

Then Ingwe grabbed him roughly. 'That girl is not to be spoken to. Do you understand? She belongs to the Mambo!'

'His wife? How can someone so beautiful belong to the lion-creature?'

'Not yet his wife. But she is promised! She is preparing for marriage.' His eyes were dark as well water. 'Now follow me! The Mambo wishes to see you.'

Maji glanced towards the stone platform. The figure had gone. The daggers of stone pointed up at the dark sky.

'I don't want to see him.'

'It's not for you to choose!'

They passed between dancing bodies, out of the enclosure and through the crowded meeting place. The air smelt of smoke and sweat. Then they left the terraces of huts behind and climbed a steep path between huge rocks. Here the air was fresher. Dark shapes of bats swooped and squeaked around their ears. A baboon barked. Giant boulders stood dark against a sky sprinkled with stars.

They came to a place where the path was so narrow that Maji had to twist sideways. In the valley below, he could see the flares of torches and fires. They hovered like swarms of fireflies. Drumbeats vibrated in the still air.

His own heart made drumbeats in his ears.

Why did the Mambo want to see him?

What would he ask? What would he say?

He followed Ingwe through an intricate weaving of passages. They passed through a narrow entrance. On the other side was an enclosed area open to the stars. Ingwe stepped forward and spoke to some guards. In the flickering torchlight Maji counted more clay dwellings than the fingers of both hands. They were patterned with dark and light earth. Along the tops of the walls were the stone turret shapes he'd seen before.

'Do not speak to the Mambo unless spoken to,' Ingwe

warned. 'Keep your eyes fixed on the ground to show respect.'

'Stop!' A voice rang out from the shadows. 'Turn around!' the voice commanded.

'Turn!' Ingwe hissed under his breath.

Maji turned slowly so that his back was to the voice.

'Turn again!' A man stepped into the torchlight on to a raised clay platform.

Ingwe bowed. He nudged Maji to bow as well.

The man was dressed in a white robe. Maji kept his eyes down. The platform was decorated with the outline of three crocodiles. On the ground at his feet was a display of metal gongs and adzes and gold spearheads. The edges of the spearheads were so finely cut, they appeared useless. Around them were carved animals covered with thinly hammered-out sheets of gold. Maji had never seen so much gold.

In a circle outside all of these were large cowrie shells the size of a man's fist. What long journey had brought them so far from the sea?

Could this be the Great Mambo who had worn the lion mask? Surely not! He slid his glance a little higher without raising his head. The man's arms were bound with cuffs of gold and around his shoulders he wore a cloak of twisted genet tails. Pieces of turtle shell hung on a leather thong from his neck. They looked fresh and new.

'So you are the one who calls water from the earth?'

Maji slid his eyes down quickly. The man's hands! The Mambo was wearing Tamu's ring! There could only be one ring of such intricate silverwork set with two such stones. What right had he to wear the stolen ring?

He felt his fingers clench. But before he could move, the Mambo spoke again.

'You are the one with the stick that can make rivers run, wells fill, and lakes appear.'

Maji's mouth was suddenly as dry as the driest riverbed. How could Ingwe have told him all these things?

'Can you do that?'

'I . . . I . . .' The words stuck to his lips.

'He says he can!' It was Bere's voice.

'You will be tested,' the Mambo said. 'You must find water as you've promised!'

Maji bit his lip. What had he promised? Or rather . . . what had Ingwe and Bere promised?

'Remember one thing! Your water must come from the earth, not from the sky! You are forbidden to direct the Spirit of Rain. Only *I* may dance the Rain Dance!'

Hmm! Had the Mambo's rain dance worked? Maji was tempted to look up to see whether rain clouds covered the stars.

'Tomorrow your stick must speak!'

Maji bit his lip again. 'But . . .'

'Great Mambo, Conqueror of Enemies!' Ingwe stepped forward and bowed. 'The boy has had a long journey. He needs time to allow his stick to speak.'

'Time?'

Ingwe nodded.

'How much is needed?'

'A moon perhaps . . . ?'

'A moon is a long time!'

'Yes, Great Mambo but . . .'

'Very well. I will give him the time of one moon. Let his stick call water soon! My Kingdom thirsts.' He dismissed them with a wave.

Ingwe nudged Maji to walk backwards for a few steps.

'Now prove your magic powers!' Bere whispered fiercely behind him.

Thirteen

Maji slept alone that night. The herders did not return from the cattle pastures. Nor the next night, nor the next. Day after day the sun made a fat blister in the sky. Wherever he looked, he saw leafless trees that cracked and snapped as he pulled at a branch.

The Mambo had not understood. His stick didn't call water. It was water that called the stick. And the stick answered by turning in his hand. No amount of walking around with the stick could make water come if the water wasn't already hidden under the ground.

He knew this. And Ingwe knew it as well. That's why he'd asked the Mambo for more time.

If he found water, he would ask for freedom to return to the sea. But first he had to be sure he still held the power. His stick needed to be tested. He had to find the small spring halfway up the ridge that Ingwe had told him of. He had to make sure the stick still turned in his hand.

Across the dry ground of the meeting place, old men sat dreaming under the thorns of the big muunga tree in the heat of the day. A few others crouched playing a game with small pebbles in holes in the ground. It looked like the game of bao Tamu had played. Young girls walked past with pots balancing on their heads, their skin so dark, the sharp sunlight seemed to shatter against their arms and shoulders. Against the hut walls in narrow rims of shade, women were weaving stories into baskets with dyed grass. Older women were snaking coils of clay on to pots held between their feet. Around them babies crawled and played in the dust and were scooped up as they squabbled. And dogs lay panting in the sun tormented by flies.

Maji felt their eyes on him as he passed. He felt strange. Different. Apart from them all. They were part of the Kingdom. He was separate from them. He had to find water.

When he saw a few young girls filling their water pots near a patch of reeds, he knew he was at the right place. He stepped aside and waited while they chatted and teased each other. When the pots were full, they adjusted the plaited grass rings on their heads and lifted the pots on to them. Then they walked back in line along the path and giggled as they passed him.

Now there was only one girl left behind. The Mambo's promised wife. The girl he was forbidden to speak to.

She knelt down between the reeds and sucked at the water. Then she cupped water in her hands and combed it through her hair with her fingertips. Her hair was plaited into thin braids. The white disc of a moon-shell was tied to her forehead. Its spirals had worn smooth and flat. A string of minute cowrie shells clung to her neck. Drops of water lay trapped and glistening in them.

Suddenly he longed for some shells from the sea to give her as well.

She sat back on her haunches and looked directly at him.

His throat felt dry. His skin prickled. He had never looked straight into the eyes of a girl before.

She laughed as if sensing his unease. 'The spring is forbidden when the girls are filling their gourds. Only after we've left may others come to the water.'

'The girls have left.'

She smiled. Her eyes were dark with mischief. 'But I haven't. Did you stay to watch me?'

He looked down at his feet. 'I came to test my water-stick.'

'Why?'

'To see whether its magic will work.'

She burst out laughing. 'So it's true what the girls say!'

'What do they say?'

'They sing about you in their songs.'

'What? What do they sing?'

'They sing about you speaking to sticks.' Her eyes gleamed.

He refused to answer.

She laughed again. 'Only bones and special plants and things of the N'anga have magic that can speak with spirits.'

'My stick has magic.'

'What sort?'

'It shows where water is.'

'How does it work?'

'It twists in my hand when water is nearby.'

'There's water here between the reeds. Show me!'

He felt sorry he'd spoken so freely. If he showed his power, it might become less.

'Your stick can't have magic if you won't show me!' she challenged.

He kept silent.

'It's an ordinary stick. If it had real magical powers, you would be the N'anga.'

Who was she to decide what his stick could or could not do? And what was this N'anga in any case?

'I'm a water diviner!' He stood a little straighter, waiting for her to be impressed.

She flicked drops of water into the air and watched them turn to bright beads of light.

'One who finds water,' he added since she hadn't asked.

She laughed. 'I know what a diviner is. You could never be a water diviner.'

'Why?'

'Water diviners have to have courage.'

He bit at his lip.

Her eyes challenged his. 'If you have courage, show me the power of your stick.'

He stared back. Then slowly he began walking towards her with the stick gripped in front of him. What if it didn't work? His knuckles turned pale from holding so tightly. After a moment he felt it twitch. As he relaxed, it flipped over.

'Tchh!' She clicked her tongue. 'You moved it yourself!'

'No! The water called it.'

'Yes? Well then let me try!'

She reached towards the stick. He pulled back from her. One of the prongs tore.

'What?' Maji blinked and looked and blinked again.

She jumped back with the broken piece dangling in her hand. They were both silent. Looking at each other. Not daring to speak.

Then she flung it from her hands as if it were a piece of hot coal.

'What?' He stared down at the broken piece. 'What . . . ?'

But before he could find the words, she turned and ran down the path.

He stood with the sun beating a dark blindness into his head. What now? What now? He wanted to yell out after her. But she'd gone. All he had was this confusion inside his head. One moment the stick had been working, the next it lay in the dust at his feet like a snake with its back broken. His power gone! Just like that! What now? The stick was his only bargaining power.

What if the Mambo found out?

Damn the girl! He glanced about. Had someone seen? He snatched up the broken stick and quickly tucked it out of sight under his cloth wrap. Now he would have to face Ingwe and explain.

Suddenly there was a commotion up ahead. Oxen bellowed. Goats bleated. Dogs barked. A huge waterfall of dust tumbled down from the far ridge. It was the herders returning at last from the cattle-post.

He didn't want to see either Mufudzi or Jee or any of the other herders. Not now. Soon enough they would know about the broken stick. And Mufudzi would be full of challenges.

He turned quickly and followed a path that led through thick, thorny bush away from the Kingdom.

Damn! Damn the girl!

PART FOUR
THE HAKATA

Fourteen

He kicked loose stones that lay along the path. He snapped branches as he went.

What now? How would he find water without the stick? Why had he shown her? She had challenged him. When she spoke of courage, wasn't that a challenge? Who was she to challenge? Yet he should never have shown her the stick.

It was suddenly very quiet. The noise of the Kingdom had disappeared. Maji stopped to listen. Heat drew out the smell of bitter herbs. The only sound to break the silence was the sharp *krik! krik!* of pods splitting and bursting open in the dry air.

Suddenly a shrivelled man stood in the path ahead of him. Tufts of black hair sprouted from his head-dress. Gourds and seed rattles were tied to his arms and legs. As he moved they made a soft *shrr shrr* sound like wind stirring dry leaves on a tree.

Maji was too scared to look into his face. He kept his eyes level with the man's necklace. It was hung with pieces of glass, small bones, a root and a shrivelled thing with claws on it.

'Why are you here at the cave of the N'anga?' The man's voice rasped.

So this was the N'anga!

The man poked and tapped the ground in front of him with a stick.

Maji looked down. He had six toes on his left foot.

'You've brought no grain. No calf. Not even a chicken!'

Maji stood rooted and silent as a tree stump.

The man's claw fingers groped towards his face.

He shrank from the touch. He wanted to be gone from this place.

'Wait!' the man grabbed at his shoulder. 'I see you!'

Maji slid a glance upwards. The tufts of hair cast dark shadows across the man's face. A strange white skin covered both eyes. The man was blind.

'You are the boy with special powers. In our Kingdom, only the Mambo and the N'anga have special powers!'

Maji swallowed hard.

'Your silence questions my power! What have you brought me?'

He shook his head. 'Nothing. I have nothing.'

'You have nothing except a stick. Where is your stick?'

The white milky eyes stared straight past him. The claw fingers groped at his shoulder.

'Wait! I must fetch my hakata. I must consult with the spirits to see how great your power is.'

The seed rattles rustled as the man disappeared through a cleft between some huge boulders. A six-toed footprint was left behind in the sand.

Maji wanted to run but his feet had grown roots.

The N'anga returned with something wrapped in a dark skin. He crouched down and smoothed dust away from a place on the ground that was already hard from use. Then he set down the skin parcel.

Maji leant forward. Pieces that looked like knucklebones fell out together with a few shells, then four long pieces of carved bone.

The N'anga slithered the pieces together in his hand. Then he scattered them on to the skin. He stared straight ahead and chanted, 'They have fallen in a heap. They have fallen in a heap.' His fingers groped over the patterns on the bone pieces. 'The throw says the man . . . and the crocodile! The man! And the crocodile!'

Maji glanced down. There was a carving of a crocodile on one of the pieces of bone. On another was a zigzag line. The other two had fallen with their blank sides upwards.

The N'anga's eyes stared past Maji. He rubbed one of the pieces with the tips of his fingers. 'The crocodile is the sign of the Mambo. It's the hakata for an old and powerful man. This one here, with the markings of a winding snake, is the sign of a young man. See!' He held it out. 'The snake of fertility. Like you!'

Maji looked down at the zigzag pattern wriggling over the piece of bone. He chewed his lip. 'So . . .?'

'Will the snake conquer the crocodile?' The N'anga laughed a strange harsh laugh. 'Will the young man conquer the Mambo?'

Maji kept silent.

The N'anga shook his head. 'I'll say no more. Just this
. . . your power is not lost. It remains yours. Even though
the stick is broken.'

How had he known about the broken stick?

'But you must find a new stick.'

'Where?' Maji managed to ask.

The N'anga shook his head. 'You have paid nothing.
Nothing more can be told. But I warn you. Be careful!
The girl belongs to the Mambo.'

The white skin made his eyes expressionless. His
mouth closed in a tight hard line. Maji knew no more
words would be prised from his lips. He glanced down
at the four, carved hakata lying on the skin with the
other bones. There were so many questions.

Fifteen

A smell of dust and dung in the air and there was the restless sound of cattle coming from the cattle enclosure. Perhaps the boy called Jee would be there. He would know where to find Ingwe.

Jee was leaning against the pole fence of the cattle boma with some of the other herders. He was playing a reed pipe with holes cut into it. As he blew, his long thin fingers covered the holes and the air was filled with whistling sounds.

When he saw Maji, he stopped playing. 'We're back!' he announced with a smile, then began the greeting Maji was beginning to know. 'I see you. If you are well, then I am well.'

'Hmm!'

Jee blinked at him. 'You don't seem well! You look worried.'

'I have seen . . .' Maji quickly checked himself. Should he tell about the N'anga and the hakata?

'What?'

Maji shrugged. 'Nothing.'

'What have you seen?'

Mufudzi clicked his tongue loudly and looked around at them. 'Tch! You chatter like monkeys! Now I've lost count and must begin again. I've forgotten which names I've called.'

Maji glanced at the herd milling around inside the pole fence boma. 'How can you know all their names?'

Mufudzi gave him a hard look. Then went on calling.

Jee smiled. 'They are called by the shape of their horns or by their colour.'

'They all look the same to me.'

Mufudzi clicked his tongue again. 'That's because you're not a herder. You know nothing. See! One has a bent horn. Another a horn that hangs down. Or red marks on the forelegs. Or a patch of white on the face. We know them all by name.' He tied the gate to the post with a strip of skin and nodded. 'They're all counted. Come!'

Jee slipped the reed flute into the waist of his skin cloth. 'Are you coming, Maji?'

'Where to?'

'Who knows? To hunt for the bird that will guide us to honey? To trap guinea fowl? To trick tsoko? Or play spinning beans? Let's follow Mufudzi. He always has a plan!'

Maji shook his head. 'I must find Ingwe.'

'Perhaps we'll see him. Come! Follow us some of the way.' He nudged a boy walking next to him. 'This one who walks at my side is my friend, Nungu.'

'Nungu?'

Jee nodded. 'You know the porcupine with all its quills? Well this is Nungu. He's a little fellow but prickly.

Beware of annoying him!' He dangled his arm around another boy's shoulders. 'And this one who jumps about and climbs trees like a monkey, is my friend, Tsoko. And this one who walks so quietly with the listening face is Tsinza, the little oribi. Come friends. We can show Maji some tricks!'

They walked in a line, Mufudzi up front whistling between his teeth, a few herders, then Jee with his long thin arms dangling so loosely at his sides that they seemed not to be part of him, then Nungu, Tsoko and Tsinza. Maji followed at the back, his broken stick still tucked out of sight.

When some smaller children tried to follow, Mufudzi chased them away. 'We don't want gnats buzzing around us. Go back to your mothers.'

In an open space he started digging narrow holes in the ground.

'Are you digging for roots to eat?' Maji asked.

Mufudzi looked at him as if he were one of the small children. 'Roots? You know nothing!'

'What then?'

'Does a lion bother with a hare? Who wants roots?' He took some lumps of millet porridge from a small pouch and dropped them in the holes.

'Hide in the grass. You'll see!' Jee said with a playful smile.

Mufudzi nudged him to keep quiet.

The smell of the dry grass was strong. It tickled his nose. He felt he would sneeze.

A group of speckled blue-faced guinea fowl crossed

the pathway. They began pecking around the holes. One pushed its head into a narrow hole to get at the millet. When its head stuck tight in the opening, Mufudzi dashed forward and grabbed it before it could flap free.

'It works every time!' Jee laughed.

'Every time, if you're quiet enough! And if Tsoko stands still!' Mufudzi tucked the squawking bird under his arm. 'Now you try, Maji! We need two for our cook-pot.'

Maji chewed at his bottom lip. 'I have to find Ingwe.'

'He's at his cave.' Mufudzi jerked his head in the direction of the ridge.

Maji glanced up towards the ridge. How did Mufudzi know everything?

Heat shimmered across the huge boulders. The bumpy outline was the jawbone of a huge animal. He searched the rocks. He couldn't see Ingwe's cave. But he knew somewhere up there, was the Mambo's court. And in the Mambo's court was the Mambo, wearing Tamu's ring and waiting. Waiting for him to find water.

'Be careful!' Jee touched his shoulder. 'Where the path splits, take the path to the right, not the one to the Mambo's enclosure.'

How had Jee guessed what he was thinking?

Sixteen

He followed Jee's directions until he found himself in a walled area that clung to the side of the cliff. He passed between two boulders into a dark cave. The only light came from a narrow cleft that showed a patch of sky.

His eyes took a few moments to get used to the gloom. Piles of strange things lay about. Strips of animal skin splattered with dark stains that looked like blood. Small leather bags stitched and decorated with rooster spurs and feathers. Iron bars hammered into the rock. Twisted leather thongs hanging from them.

A shudder ran through him. Was it something to do with the N'anga?

'What are you doing?'

He spun around. 'What?'

'What are you doing in Ingwe's cave?'

In the darkness he saw the pale white circle of a moon-shell. It was the promised wife.

'Why do you creep up on me?'

She remained in the shadow. 'Sshh! Ingwe mustn't find me here. No one must see us.'

'If no one must see us, why are you here?'

'Don't be so cross! In any case I go where I please. I know secret paths. I can disappear and reappear just like that!' She snapped her fingers.

'Aren't you supposed to stay with the wives?'

'The wives never do anything in a hurry. They braid each other's hair and jabber jabber. That's all they do all day. I can dart away as fast as a fish swims and be back before they know I've gone.'

'If you're found out?'

She looked hard at him. Then laughed. 'I won't be.'

'You might!'

She shrugged. 'I'll trick them. They're easy to trick.'

'How?'

'I'll tell them I had to fetch something for the oldest wife. Some beads or a feather for her hair. The younger wives daren't challenge me. The oldest wife is not to be disobeyed.'

She leant up against a rock with both hands at her sides and sighed. 'I can always escape from them. In any case I'm the Mambo's favourite.'

He couldn't see her expression. 'Why did you come here?'

She drew patterns in the sand with her toe. She dotted and made squiggles and finished with a swoop, then stared down as if the drawing would give the answer.

'Well . . . ?'

'To find you.'

'Why?'

'I wanted to say sorry . . .'

'What . . . ?'

'Sorry . . . about the stick.'

'Sorry . . . ? Sorry . . . ?' He stared back at her. In the shadow it was impossible to see her face. 'You think you can say sorry and everything is fine again? Just sorry! Sorry about the stick! And I must be happy with that!'

'Why do you get so cross?'

'What?'

'Cross.'

'Me . . . ?'

'Yes! You're always complaining.'

'I'm not!'

'You are!'

'This is stupid. I don't have to answer you.'

She sighed and clicked her tongue. 'See! You're cross again!'

'I'm not!' Maji felt his skin prickle with irritation. 'What do you want with me?'

She looked down at her drawing but didn't speak. She added a few more dots with her toe.

'Go back to your secret paths and your hair-braiding! Leave me alone!'

'I want to tell you something.'

'What?'

'I thought you were brave to visit the N'anga.'

'What . . . ?'

'You were brave. And you *do* have courage.'

He stared back at her. Was she smiling?

Suddenly she pushed away from the rock and strode past him. She stopped for a moment in the bright sunlight outside the cave. Her eyes flashed as she looked back. 'I like that!'

'What?'

'Courage!'

Then she was gone.

Maji's head buzzed. He wanted to run after her and shake her. Who was she to tell him whether he was cross or not! Or for that matter whether he had courage or not! And how had she known about the N'anga? Jee was right. Nothing stayed secret. But if she wanted to believe he had chosen to visit the N'anga and that he was brave, then let her!

She was strange. Everything in this Kingdom was strange. And now at his feet in the soft sand was a drawing of a bird with feathers and a wing . . . or was it a fish with scales and a fin? It was hard to tell.

Beyond the cave, some falcons were drifting above the ridge. They made circle upon circle against the colourless sky. He caught sight of Ingwe standing on top of a huge termite mound. He was whirling a thong over his head. A dead bird was tied to it.

As Maji walked nearer, Ingwe held up his arm for him to stand back. Then he called with a high-pitched whistling sound, 'Come, my beauties! Fly low! See what I have. Bring this down and you know the reward. Something far juicier.'

Suddenly a bird swooped. It was like watching a stone fall from the sky. Maji felt wing-beats stir the air around his face.

'Rani! I see you by the moult of your first feathers.'

Ingwe swung the lure carefully. It trailed just in front of the falcon. As the bird sped forward to catch it, he snatched the thong out of reach. The falcon swerved swiftly upwards and circled high again.

Ingwe whistled. 'Come, Rani! This is a game we must learn to play together. Learn not to be fearful. Listen to my call.'

The falcon flew low again. This time Ingwe allowed her to strike the lure. She made the strike on the wing, sinking her claws firmly into the dead bird.

'Gently! Gently! Take the circle I lead you on. Now, lower! Don't drop the prey. There! Safe on the ground! See! It's all trust!'

The falcon tore off bits of flesh from the lure.

'Come!' Ingwe whistled softly and held out his arm. It was bound with leather. On top of the bindings he placed a piece of raw meat.

The falcon hesitated. Her white throat and spotted chest throbbed. Then she gave a screech and flew to perch on his outstretched hand. She made a quick grab at the fresh meat. Just as quickly, Ingwe snatched two small leather straps that were attached to her legs with his other hand, so that she couldn't fly up again.

'See . . .' he spoke without taking his eyes off the bird, '. . . it's done with great patience. Maziso has trained her well while I've been away. She's grown. Her chest is expanding. Soon she'll bring down her own prey. Approach quietly or she'll frighten without her hood.'

The bird gave sharp sidelong glances. From close up it seemed even more fearsome. Maji kept an eye on the sharp talons. No wonder Ingwe's wrists were bound. Of course! Now he understood the scratches and scars on his arms.

Ingwe slipped a leather covering over the bird's head. It was tufted with feathers and a rooster spur, like the ones Maji had seen in the cave.

'This will calm her.'

Then he tied her thongs to a metal perch that was driven into a large wooden frame resting on the ground. There were five more metal perches attached to it.

The hooded bird sat quite still.

'Who is Maziso?'

'A boy who looks after the birds while I'm away. They need to be exercised to keep up their strength and ability. One day he'll be a fine falconer!'

Maji felt a little stab below his ribs. Given the chance, he too could be a fine falconer.

Ingwe tied another small dead bird on the end of the thong and began swinging it above his head again. He brought down four more falcons in the same way, calling them each by name. Urtu, Jez, Chokwadi, Duka.

It looked so easy.

Now there was only one bird left in the sky. This time Ingwe dropped the thong to the ground. He whistled. The bird came down lower, flying in huge circles.

'This is Mhepo – the Wind.' Ingwe spoke in a whisper. 'I leave him for last. Watch! He doesn't need a lure. He makes a kill perfectly. We just need to be patient. Look how he is hovering, waiting for the right prey.'

Maji watched silently. Suddenly there was a flicker as a brown-speckled hwari bird flew up from the grass. In a swoop so fast the eye couldn't hold it, Mhepo struck. He flew to perch in a tree with the bird hanging from his beak.

Ingwe whistled. Mhepo immediately brought the quarry to the ground a few paces away from Ingwe's feet. Ingwe offered his wrist and whistled again.

Maji held his breath. Would the bird leave the quarry and obey?

The falcon eyed them both. Then he dropped the hwari bird and with a swoop flew up on to Ingwe's wrist-bindings and took the piece of meat.

'Ahee-yah, Mhepo! Ndatenda. Thank you. You haven't lost your speed. Or your trust.' Ingwe gripped the leg bindings firmly.

The falcon answered with a noisy *kazikk-zikk-zikk!* and a bobbing movement. His head almost touched his talons and his tail feathers lifted and fanned out.

'Watch now!' Ingwe moved his other hand. 'A well-trained falcon follows the falconer's hand with its eyes and flaps its wings as if wanting to fly. Always ready to obey.'

'Who taught you these things?'

'A man of the desert. A trader. A true falconer who used birds for hunting,' Ingwe replied as he hooded the falcon.

'How do you choose a bird?'

'A hunting bird has to be firm in flight. Patient when carried. Properly fed. An underfed bird is weak. She flies unwillingly. At the first chance she'll settle in a tree or on the ground. And an overfed bird isn't interested in the lure. She circles lazily. You can call but she won't follow commands.'

'How do you know whether she's underfed or too fat?'

'By touching the breastbone under the feathers.' Ingwe guided Maji's hand. 'Here. Feel.'

Maji kept a sharp eye on the long talons as he fumbled through the feathers. His fingers were clumsy.

'If the bone stands out too sharply, the bird is too thin. If the bone can hardly be felt, it's too fat.' He tied the bird to the last empty perch on the frame. Then stepped into the middle of the frame, pulled some straps over his shoulders and hoisted it carefully so that none of the falcons lost their balance. He began to walk.

Maji picked up three dead hwari birds that were lying on the ground. Only small, bloodied patches showed where their necks had been broken.

Seventeen

At the cave, Ingwe piled dry sticks on top of some smouldering ash and blew the fire to life. Tendrils of flame began to curl upwards. Then they sat in silence with just the soft *pluk pluk* sound of Ingwe's fingers tearing out the hwari feathers. Fine wisps floated in front of Maji's face as he watched the edges of the earth lose shape and night creep in.

Ingwe spoke first. 'Our ancestors are here tonight!'

Maji glanced towards him. 'How do you know?'

Ingwe took a log and began beating down the coals. The glow of the fire seeped out and lost itself in the dusk. He laid the three hwari in a hard-baked clay pot and placed some leaves on top. Then he settled the pot in the fire, twisting it so that the coals surrounded it. Only when the job was done did he answer.

'I feel them.'

'How?'

'Through the falcons.'

'The falcons?'

Ingwe nodded. 'Falcons are messengers of our ancestors. They're the spirits of all who have gone before us. They fly up and take messages to the Great Mwari in the Sky.'

'Who is he, this Great Mwari?'

'His voice is heard in thunder. His kindness is felt in rain. His throne is surrounded by stars.'

Maji glanced up at the myriad stars that filled the sky like dust. Was this Mwari who lived amongst the stardust the same as Allah?

'In the Kingdom, they honour Mambos of the past by making special falcon carvings. The carvings are called Birds of God. Each carving marks the spirit of a Mambo who has died.'

'How can it mark his spirit?'

'Each one is different. Each Mambo must be remembered individually.'

'And then . . . ?'

'Ancestral spirits fly up to heaven as falcons. They plead with the Great Mwari on our behalf. When the Mambo dances the Rain Dance he's talking to the spirits.'

Maji looked out across the valley. The air stirring against his face carried the tang of dry herbs but no smell of rain. The Rain Dance hadn't worked. Above the ridge the moon rose huge and full and cast strange shadows over the stone walls. Dark shapes of bats swooped around them. A baboon barked and was answered somewhere below.

It was time to speak of the broken stick. But he held back. He couldn't say the promised wife had broken it. Instead he asked, 'Who built the first walls?'

'Who planted the first tree?'

Maji kept silent.

'Ancestors taught these people in dreams. The higher the walls, the closer the Mambo is to the Great Mwari in the Sky. For this reason the Mambo's enclosure and the sacred place with the falcon carvings are on the highest ridge.'

'Why do you say *these* people and not *my* people?'

'They're not my people. I come from a place far from here.'

'Where?'

'From the Great River. A river that never stops flowing. A river greater than all rivers. We lived where mukwa and muunga trees grow taller than stone buildings, on an island in the middle of this Great River.'

Maji thought of when his stick had first found water on the journey. Ingwe had said he knew about water signs. So this was it! Now he tried to imagine the Great River on Tamu's map. A wide winding snake with its head in the sea and its tail stretching far into the land where the sun went down.

'How did you live?'

'We lived as we always lived. We fished for bream in the quiet side-waters. We hunted hippos with spears on long ropes. And we planted the donje bush on the riverbanks. When the seeds burst, we collected the tufts and spun thread to weave cloth. From traders we learnt to dye the thread different colours. Red and yellow from ochre. And even blue. The blue dye we traded for. It's very costly.'

Maji nodded. He knew this blue indigo. It was from Musqat.

'The women washed the coloured threads in pools next to the river.'

He glanced at Ingwe. The firelight had made his face soft. In the reflection of Ingwe's eyes, he saw pools swirling with rust and ochre and indigo.

'Then why are you here now?'

'I know how to trade.'

'Yes, but your people? What happened to them?'

Ingwe was slow to answer. 'The Mambo wanted cloth. He needed thread from the donje bush. He wanted more and more for his Kingdom. He is a man of fire. My people were pools of calm water.'

'And so?'

'Fire surrounds pools. It dries them up.'

Maji stared out over the moon-washed valley. The huge boulders along the ridge had turned into domes of silver. He thought of the domes of Kilwa's mosque. Silver in the moonlight.

'I too have given up my ancestors,' he whispered. 'I've left them far behind.'

'No one gives up his ancestors. They come into our lives like guests who need no invitation.'

'No! You're mistaken. My ancestors are lost to me.'

'Why do you think this?'

'I'm here alone. Far from the sea.'

'No. You're not alone. The gift of finding water is from your ancestors. The spirit of your ancestors helped you guard your father's grave. It was their spirit that helped fight the poison of the arrow. Then at the rapids, they helped you save the boat. Your ancestors speak in you.'

'But why?'

'The earth is not our land. Our lives start before we are born. There is no real beginning or end. We are bound by the earth for a short time. Then our spirits are set free again.'

'Has Tamu's spirit been set free?'

'Yes, Tamu's spirit has returned to the sea. His grave is washed by the waves. Only when returned to the sea is the spirit of a sea creature truly free.'

'Is that why you left the turtles' heads on stakes?'

Ingwe nodded. 'It shows kindness. The heads will decay and drop to the sand and be washed back into the sea.'

Maji eyed him in the darkness. 'And my spirit? What will happen to my spirit? It has no resting place here.'

'It'll be near water. You've shown that's where you belong. As water calls your stick, so water will call you. But first you must find it for the Mambo. I have pleaded once more on your behalf. He has allowed you extra time. Another moon.'

'Another moon?'

'Yes . . . but you must find a new stick.'

Maji glanced back sharply. How had he known? He too heard news faster than drumbeats.

'You must find a new stick, before it's too late.'

'If I find water will the Mambo allow me to return to Kilwa?'

'The Mambo is a dry riverbed.'

'What . . . ?'

'He soaks up everything. Nothing escapes him.'

'But if the Mambo demands more and more, the power will no longer be mine!'

'You've no choice. His power is great and his soldiers strong. You've seen Bere. He doesn't carry his name for nothing.'

'Bere . . . the hyena?'

'Yes.'

'What of Bere?'

'He has the jaws of a hyena. He doesn't stop until the last bone is crunched.'

'If the stick is broken, how will I find water?'

'Find another. The stick isn't important. It's you. The power comes from you. Another green stick will work just as well.'

They ate the soft flesh of the cooked hwari birds. Then they sat for a long time around the warm ashes looking out over the valley and watching the moon float higher and higher.

A leopard slipped across the plain. Its outline turned to silver. Its whiskers trapped the moonlight. In the stillness, Maji sensed the soft pad of its paws against the earth. For a moment the leopard hesitated and looked back. He held his breath. Its yellow eyes locked with his. A deep grunt came from far back in its throat. Then it turned and padded forward again with its head carried low and disappeared in the dry grass.

Maji turned to meet Ingwe's eyes across the fire. He sensed a friendship between them now. A friendship that had grown without saying this is so . . . or that is so.

PART FIVE
BIRDS OF PREY

Eighteen

The beer was making Maji's head funny. It was the Chapungu Ceremony. And Jee had said it was important to drink beer because it was an important ceremony.

Maji held on to his legs to keep himself from floating into the air. The wall at his back was drifting away. Huge black birds tall as men, swaggered around him. Red-pointed beaks wanted to tear into him. Wings beat around his face.

And now where was Jee? And the other herders? Where were they? Mufudzi? Nungu? Tsoko? And Tsinza?

Then he saw Jee up against the opposite wall. He wished he would stop grinning and drifting about. 'Stand still, Jee!' he begged. 'What do these birds want?'

The bird faces leant towards him and hissed, 'We are the Chapungu-men! We're the bateleurs. We sweep the heavens. Our eyes find the weak. Our beaks tear them apart.'

The air filled with wing sounds. He tried to scramble up. He lifted his arms to protect his face. Feathers brushed his hands. Beaks snapped. He sensed a single tall dark shape in front of him.

'Maji!' The bird-shape called his name. Below the red-pointed beak, part of a thick scar showed across the left cheek.

His legs that had wanted to float before now went stiff like a dog's when a snake is in the path. His head was full of scared thoughts. He squeezed his eyes tight shut to make the bird shape go away. But when he opened them again, Bere was still in front of him.

Bere lifted the feathered headdress. He came up close.

Maji shrunk back from the smell of him. He wanted him gone.

'You haven't found water yet? Where is your power? Remember, I have the power to call up the hiss of a cobra or the bite of a hyena! I have seen you with the Mambo's promised wife.'

When? Maji wanted to ask but the words choked in his throat.

'Watch out! You are the short hare. And the short hare cannot eat the tall grass! Be warned!'

The voice sent shivers through his bones. Why was it that Bere had such power to terrify him?

A horn sounded. Bere disappeared between the other Chapungu-men. They settled like a flock of giant black birds under the muunga tree. At Maji's feet was one of Bere's feathers. It lay dark and silent on the hard ground. What omen was this?

Iron struck iron. Everyone stood silent. Then the Mambo appeared. His robes were blinding white. Gold neckbands and bracelets reflected back a hundred suns. Women bowed and shuffled backwards on their knees, sweeping the dust in his path with their fingers, their voices high-pitched in the back of their throats as they called out praises.

The Mambo was followed by a long line of wives. They wore wraps threaded with gold. Their hair glistened with beads. Maji glanced from one to the other, searching for the face of the promised wife. Where was she? He hadn't seen her since the day at Ingwe's cave.

Then from the corner of his eye there was a shimmer. He caught his breath. She was finer and more slender-waisted than any of the others. The string of cowries clung to her neck. The moon-shell was tied on her forehead. She walked lightly through the sunlight in the still air. He felt sure there were times when both her feet were off the ground. There was laughter and brightness in her face. As if she knew she was the most beautiful of all the women.

It was no longer possible to be angry with her for breaking his water-stick.

Across the crowd he saw Ingwe watching as well. Why was Ingwe always so close by whenever she appeared?

Then the Mambo held up a flaming cloth on a long pole and called out, 'I rule with the power that comes from my forefathers! The power without beginning!'

The praise-singers echoed back, 'You rule with the power that comes from your forefathers! The power without beginning!'

The Mambo led the procession to where the Chapungu-men were standing three abreast in a column. Each man came forward with an oiled cloth tied to a stick. As the Mambo lit each one, he called out, 'Take my power throughout the Kingdom!'

'Aa-eee! Aa-yah! Aa-eee! Aa-yah! We take your power with us!' they chanted.

Maji caught hold of Jee. 'What's happening?'

'The fire must be taken throughout the Kingdom. When the Chapungu-men reach a village, every fire in the village has to be put out. Not even a single cooking fire must be left burning. Those who wish for fire must come to receive it from the Mambo's flame.'

'Why?'

'As a sign of his power. From this he judges whether people are obedient to him.'

'If not? What happens?'

'Their food and belongings are burnt or taken. The people are brought back here. Put to work in the stone quarry as his slaves. Or else they're killed.'

Maji shuddered. This was the darkness he had felt creeping up on him that night under the musimbiti trees. This was the fire-power. This was how the Mambo ruled such a large Kingdom.

The air was filled with a smell of burning. M'biras twanged.

First the Mambo's wives came forward to receive the flame from the Chapungu-men. Then it was the turn of the other women of the Kingdom. Some strode forward briskly, eager for their turn. Others came with their heads bowed and their feet shuffling. Some with babies tied to their backs. Others with young children at their sides, clutching their skin wraps. Then a long line of girls came forward to receive the flame as well. All of them held up sticks with oil-soaked cloths to be lit from the Chapungu-men's flames so their cooking fires could be relit.

Now the wives began to dance. They chanted and waved torches. The dance became faster and faster. Wraps swirled in the dust. Brilliant cloths became streamers of coloured sunlight. Gold bands glittered against dark skins. Shapes of people turned to liquid.

Then the Chapungu-men marched forward. They held their torches high and bowed their bird heads as they passed the Mambo.

He stood upright and silent, like a shaft of stone against the sky.

The air around the Chapungu-men shimmered in waves of heat. Against the glare, they marched towards the sun. A dark moving mass that seemed to hover in a circle of light just above the ground. Like a huge swarm of attacking bees. Then they disappeared against the light, taking their fire-sticks and their power with them.

The youngest promised wife passed close enough for Maji to smell the warmth of her skin. He longed to whisper her name. But he didn't know it.

As she passed, she stooped as if the edge of her wrap had caught at her heels. For a brief moment her dark eyes looked straight into his. She laughed as she rearranged the folds of cloth, as if daring him to speak to her.

His stomach twisted. She confused him. It was as if there were some secret between them. Yet he didn't know what it was.

Then she walked on lightly again through the smoky air, with brightness in her face and both feet off the ground. She was a fly-away girl.

As he turned, he saw Jee grinning at him. And further away through the crowd, he caught Ingwe watching him as well. What had they both seen?

That night the herders jostled around the fire with sticks and Tsoko jumped about from group to group. 'Who will be a Chapungu-man? Who will be a Chapungu-man?' he chanted.

They hit their sticks as hard as they could against an opponent's stick and tried to drive him by sheer force across a line drawn in the dust. No one challenged Mufudzi. He sat with a small group of boys who had already won their fights.

In this group Mufudzi was already a Chapungu-man.

Nineteen

Maji sat waiting for Jee at the meeting place on the ridge next to the red termite mound.

Down below in the valley he could see children playing in pathways between the huts and men in the meeting place playing games of bao. Far in the distance across the fields the women were busy hoeing. Their songs floated up to him and echoed gently from ridge to ridge.

There seemed to be calm in the Kingdom now . . . now that the Chapungu–men had left. But it felt like the calm between gusts of wind in a storm. As if suddenly from nowhere the wind would swoop down and tear at the sails again and the waves would rise up and swallow him.

In the distance he saw Jee coming slowly up the path with his long fingers playing over the holes of his mutoriro reed. Damn! Mufudzi was with him! He had wanted to be alone with Jee but Mufudzi always had to meddle in everything.

'Why have you taken so long?'

Jee went on playing but Mufudzi gave him a scornful

look. 'Unlike you, we are busy. We don't walk around looking for sticks all day. When the sun rises, it's milking time. Then it's time to drive the cattle to the grazing place. Then it's time to drive them to the watering place. Then it's time to drive them back to the boma. Then they have to be milked again. In between we birth the calves. We chase away jackals. And we search for cows that have strayed.'

Jee stopped playing and laughed. 'You forgot something, Mufudzi!'

'What?'

'We sing to the cows.' He tucked his mutoriro reed into the leather thong around his waist.

'You sing to them?' Maji looked from one to the other. Were they teasing him?

'Don't you know?' Mufudzi sighed and spoke as if he was explaining something to a small child.

Maji shook his head.

'Every cow has its own milking song. When they hear you singing their song, they know to come out of the herd to be milked.'

Maji wasn't sure whether to believe him. Jee was scratching delicately in the sandy hollow of an ant-lion's trap with a piece of dry grass.

Mufudzi pushed him aside. 'That's not the way to tickle an ant-lion out of its hole. You have to tease it with a real ant.' He picked up an ant and dropped it into the hollow. As it struggled to climb out, two ugly dark claws poked out and in a quick flash, the ant-lion snatched its prey and disappeared again.

'See!'

Maji stood up impatiently. 'Tchh! This is not a time for ant-lions. Are you coming with me, Jee?'

'Where to?'

'To the Motelekwe.'

Mufudzi glanced up from the rock he was stretched out on with lazy eyes. 'It's a long way. Why should we go there?'

'I need another green stick. And you were not invited, Mufudzi. Jee, are you coming?'

'Why must you go all the way to the river?' Mufudzi insisted.

'The stick has to have sap. The trees here are like old bones. A dry stick won't work.'

'If you have magic power, you have magic power! What does it matter if you use a green stick or a dry stick?'

'Water can't twist a dry stick!'

'It's too hot.' Mufudzi sighed and rolled over on to his stomach and pretended to be asleep.

Maji turned away. He wasn't going to beg. 'I'll go on my own.'

Jee nudged Mufudzi with his foot. 'Come on! We can swim.'

Mufudzi jumped up. 'Yes, we'll swim at the Motelekwe pools,' he announced as if he himself had just had the idea.

Shavi-shavi birds with long red beaks skittered and scolded like old women in the marketplace. *Sha! tja! tja! tja!* Heavy-billed hoto birds flew clumsily from tree to tree along the path just ahead of them. They passed between the Beroma rocks. Mufudzi stopped to poke at a dead snake. Maji began to feel the river calling him. He pushed past. He wanted to be first to see the flash of a kingfisher. First to see the water.

At the river, he stopped abruptly. In a dark pool he caught a reflection of himself. It had been many moons since he had last seen his reflection. How many? Perhaps three? Not since the dhow. Then the sea had been calm with silver flying fish leaping around. His face had been that of a boy then. Now he saw someone he hardly recognized. His hair had grown long. His shoulders were broad and muscled. The face of a young man looked back at him.

His reflection shattered as Mufudzi and Jee dived into the water next to him.

'What about crocodiles?'

'Who's scared of them!' Mufudzi chopped hard against the water so that Maji was drenched.

Their swim was more about splashing and thrashing about and pushing each other under and pretending to be attacked by crocodiles, than swimming. Afterwards they chased each other and played leopard games between the thorn trees.

The sun was high already when Maji found a branch on a tree that looked as if it could be right. It was flexible and had a deep fork.

Mufudzi eyed the stick. 'That's the mupuma tree. It grows near rivers. Why didn't you say your stick had to be from the mupuma tree?'

'I didn't know.'

'There's much you don't know!' Mufudzi narrowed his eyes. 'How can you be sure it's the right stick?'

Maji kept silent. With Mufudzi it was better to say nothing. He scraped away the small new leaves. It looked like his other stick. It was smooth and green.

Jee peered over Maji's shoulder. 'Will it work?'

Maji shrugged. He walked towards a pool. He sensed the other two watching. He clutched a branch of the fork in each hand. He closed his eyes and breathed deeply. It seemed as if he stood for a long time. A shiver passed through his arms. Suddenly the stick swung.

'That's easy!' Mufudzi's look seemed to say he was sure he could do the same.

Maji tucked the stick firmly into his girdle.

Mufudzi nodded. 'Here, there's plenty of water. At the place of stones it will be different. Tomorrow we'll see if your stick finds water away from the river.'

They lay on a flat smooth rock in the sun while the hoto birds cackled in the trees above them.

'Let's ask riddles.' Jee tugged Maji's arm. 'Here's one for you. What is the thing which once poured out cannot be gathered again?'

Mufudzi snorted. 'That's a riddle for a baby, Jee! The answer is water!'

'You weren't asked!'

'Maji's too slow! Answer this one then. The witches are dancing on thorns.'

'We all know that one! Hailstones, of course! They

bounce as they fall on the dry grass. Now it's your turn to ask, Maji.'

'What is the name of the promised wife?'

Jee laughed. 'That's not a riddle.'

'Why do you want to know, Maji?' Mufudzi turned on to his stomach and studied him from under lowered eyelids. 'You're not even supposed to look at her!'

Jee grinned. 'I watched you at the Chapungu Ceremony!'

Maji punched Jee's arm. 'Well, what is it?'

'It's Mukonikoni. The Little Dragonfly. But be careful no one catches you looking.'

'Bere looks at her!'

'That's different. Bere is the Mambo's brother,' Mufudzi said. 'He looks at whom he likes!'

Maji sat up and stared hard at him. 'Bere? The Mambo's brother? It can't be true!'

Mufudzi shrugged. 'Why do you think he has so much power?'

'But . . . ?'

'Would you like her for your wife, Maji?' Jee teased.

'Jee, you speak like a baby,' Mufudzi said scornfully. 'You know Mukonikoni is promised. There has to be the length of a spear between Mukonikoni and any boy.'

'She's promised but the other wives are jealous of her. Do you think she's beautiful, Maji?'

'Tch! Maji could never have her. He's not one of us. He hasn't been to the classes of ceremony behind the Great Wall!'

'And have you? Have you been through the Great Wall Ceremony that you can speak with such wisdom of everything here in the Kingdom?' Jee retorted sharply.

Mufudzi looked hard at Jee. 'I'm older than you. It'll soon be my turn.'

'Then you'll be a *man*! No longer a boy!' Jee teased.

'Hmmph! You've nothing but the sounds of your mutoriro in your head! We don't become men just because we've finished the classes. Some boys are never men. And if you speak so stupidly you might as well go back and live in your mother's hut and suckle milk. You'll forever be a boy.'

'And you?'

'Me? I'll be tested. We become men when we've learnt the ways of men.' He glanced scornfully down at Maji. 'You can never attend our classes. You're not one of us. In our Kingdom you'll never be a man!'

Mufudzi knew how to chafe at a sore place. Maji jumped up. 'You . . . !'

'Yes?' Mufudzi challenged. 'What?'

'I don't need your classes! I've already learnt the ways of men!'

'When?' Mufudzi drew himself up taller.

Their eyes were no longer level. Maji had to look up at Mufudzi.

'On the dhow with Tamu. And on the journey to the Kingdom with Ingwe and Bere.'

Jee nodded. 'Maji's right. He's been tested.'

'Hmmph! And how do you know if he passed the test? Were you there, Jee? Did you see?' His eyes flicked over Jee. There was silence. Only the hoto birds squabbled.

'Tomorrow Maji will be tested.' He took a step closer and squared his chest so that it almost touched Maji's. His fists were clenched. 'Tomorrow we'll fight with sticks. We'll see who's a man!' he hissed.

Maji saw himself reflected in Mufudzi's eyes. His head large. His body small. Strange-looking. His legs stretching out long and thin to the ground. He would surely lose.

Mufudzi shoved him so that he had to step backwards. Then he smiled. But it wasn't really a smile. He took a gulp from the skin pouch of sour milk he'd brought along. He wiped his mouth with the back of his hand and stared back at Maji. 'Tomorrow you'll be tested twice. Your stick must find water! And your stick must fight!'

'I can't fight with a water-stick. It bends.'

'Too scared to fight you mean!'

'I—' Maji bit back the words.

'Too scared? You too should go back to your mother and suckle milk! There's no place for babies in the herder's enclosure. We've left our mothers' huts!'

Maji tried to pull himself up a little taller. 'I'm not scared!'

'Then what?'

'It's the stick. It's not meant for fighting.'

'If you can't fight with the water-stick, find another. It's the same to me!'

Mufudzi turned and walked off. When he was a little way away, he stopped and looked back over his shoulder.

'And beware of the dragonfly! Remember the dragonfly starts life just like an ant-lion! With claws!'

Maji watched his back as he disappeared through the thick bush. Then he glanced across at Jee. 'What must I do?'

Jee shrugged. 'Don't worry.'

'But I don't even know the rules!'

'With Mufudzi you just have to stand your ground.'

Maji shook his head. 'He's much stronger than me. You know that. You saw how he stands with his shoulders pulled back.'

'You're strong too. You'll do it.' Jee opened the pouch of softened tree bark he had brought along. He shared out some sweet potatoes.

Maji bit into the sweet smoky flesh but the food gave him no comfort. He knew Jee wasn't speaking the truth. If Mufudzi was so easy to fight, why didn't the other boys ever challenge him? But he knew the answer to that one as well. Yes . . . in the herders' group Mufudzi was already a Chapungu-man.

Twenty

In the morning there was no time for Jee to show Maji anything. Mufudzi decided they should fight immediately. Lines were drawn in the sand. The centre spot was marked inside the enclosure. The other herders jostled each other for a good position.

'Choose a stick,' Mufudzi said in a careless manner. As if it did not matter to him.

Jee handed Maji a stick he had just cut.

'No, not that one! I saw you cutting it, Jee. A fighting stick has to be cut by the person who fights with it. You know the rules.'

'But Maji doesn't! And he won't know how to choose the right stick.'

'He'll learn the rules soon enough. And if he can choose a water-stick, he can choose a fighting stick.'

Some herders nodded and laughed.

Nungu stood up suddenly and glared at them. 'No! That's different! He needs help to choose a stick!'

Mufudzi spun around. 'No one asked you, Nungu! It's not your fight! Stay out of this!'

Maji thought of his counting stick. It was strong and

heavy. Would it bring him luck? 'Wait! I have a stick.'

When he brought it out from the hut he felt everyone's eyes on him.

Mufudzi reached out to examine it. Then he held it up and grinned. 'What sort of stick is this with pieces cut out of it?'

Some of the other herders jeered. Jee put his hand on Maji's shoulder. 'Don't use that one. Take my stick.'

Maji hesitated, but Mufudzi had already taken his mark in the centre. He was waiting. He held a stick stripped of bark. It looked hard and was almost as thick as his wrist.

'Come!' He beckoned with a smile. But his eyes were cold and fierce. He stepped forward, his arms held high, clutching his stick in both hands. Then he began to circle. Slowly. Slowly. It was like some strange dance. Every now and again he lunged forward as if to strike, but didn't.

Maji tried not to be distracted. He stood his ground and stared straight back into Mufudzi's eyes. What was he planning?

Suddenly Mufudzi thrust out.

He lifted both arms instinctively to fend off the blow. Their sticks knocked hard. Wood against wood. He saw Mufudzi smile as if it were as easy as milking a cow. But he knew his own arms were strong from rowing and working the dhow's sails.

The pace changed. Mufudzi began to move like a huge hunting spider with its forelegs raised in attack. He twisted and thrust, jumping forwards, then backwards again out of reach. Maji had no chance to do anything. He put up his stick to fend off the blows. The strikes were lightning fast. Faster than those of a spitting cobra. And were made with as much poison in them.

'Hit! Hit!' he heard a voice urging him. But his feet shuffled in the sand and Mufudzi's stick came down harder. The knocks echoed against his stick and sent shivers up through his arms. Dust choked him. His legs ached with the effort of trying to hold his ground. He felt his body weakening. His shoulders sagging. His hands losing their grip. Please . . . not yet! Not yet!

'Come on, Maji!' Out of the corner of his eye he caught sight of Tsoko dancing around the inner circle.

'Stand back! Tsoko!' Mufudzi hissed.

Then suddenly Maji saw Tamu in front of him. Tamu was winding his head-cloth around his head with that fast twirling movement that was almost too quick to follow. Then Maji knew what to do! Instead of grasping each end of his stick to ward off the blows, he began to twirl it in one hand above his head. Around and around.

He saw Mufudzi glance up at the stick. It was the moment to strike.

He hit hard. Mufudzi jumped back with a look of surprise.

'Yes!' It was Jee's voice.

Again he twirled the stick. This time even faster. As fast as the swirls of a whirlwind. Sweat burnt his eyes. He felt dizzy but he went on twirling. The herders yelled. Then he hit Mufudzi's stick with all the force his arms could manage. He heard his own stick crack. He felt the shudder. The next moment he was standing with one short stump in his hand. The other bit lay on the ground.

He knew he'd lost.

Jee rushed up and grabbed him. He pointed to where Mufudzi had fallen back. 'He stepped back over his own line!'

Tsoko jumped up and down. 'You've won! You've won!'

Mufudzi glanced at what was left of his line in the sand. Then he drew himself up and took a step forward and stood with his chest up against Maji's. He stayed there breathing heavily with his eyes narrow. Finally he spoke through teeth that were clenched tight. 'He hasn't won! He knows nothing about stick fighting! Nothing!' he hissed.

Some of the other herders cheered.

'He doesn't even follow the rules. He twirls the stick!'

Nungu shouldered his way between them. 'You didn't explain the rules!'

Jee nodded. 'His stick found its mark. He fought with his method. You fought with yours.'

Mufudzi glared back at them.

Nungu stood with his hands clenched stiffly at his sides. 'It was a stick fight! And you stepped back over your line!'

The others were silent as they looked from one to the other.

'It wasn't a proper fight!' Mufudzi hissed. 'Everyone knows that's not stick fighting!'

In the silence Tsinza suddenly spoke. 'Perhaps Maji should teach you his way then.' His voice was quiet but strong. Everyone turned to look at him. Then they started laughing.

Mufudzi shook his head and glared around at everyone until they were silent again. 'How can anyone fight with a stick that has pieces cut out of it? We must fight again. He must choose a proper stick.'

Jee shook his head. 'No! Maji has won! You know that!'

Maji looked down at the broken piece of stick he held. His arms were too tired to fight again. He would surely lose the next time. Yet if he chose to insist he had won, Mufudzi would never forgive him. He would make his life miserable. He had to think of something very fast.

'I'll . . . I'll . . .'

'Yes?' Mufudzi narrowed his eyes.

Maji chewed his lip.

'Yes?' Mufudzi asked again.

Tsinza looked around the circle with his large dark eyes. 'Perhaps we should decide because you both fight differently, there *is* no winner.' He put his head to one side as if thinking. 'And no loser.'

'What?' Mufudzi stared back at Tsinza. His face gleamed with sweat. 'What?' Then he spun around to face Maji again. Maji didn't dare take his eyes away. There was silence. Everyone waited.

Tsinza nodded. 'Yes. Perhaps this was to show your different ways of fighting.'

Tsoko jumped up and down. 'Yes! Yes! There's no winner and no loser!'

'There's no winner or loser!' Jee repeated.

Nungu pushed between them again. 'That's right!'

Mufudzi's eyes slipped away from Maji's. He glanced slowly around at the rest of the herders. Then he waved his stick in the air and spoke as if he had just made the decision. 'There's no winner or loser!'

The herders began nodding. 'There's no winner and no loser.' They jostled and patted each other on the back and Tsoko jumped up and down between them. In the midst of it all Tsinza stood quietly watching and across everyone's heads, Maji caught Jee grinning at him.

He lowered the piece of broken stick and felt his arms and legs go slack.

PART SIX
WATER

Twenty-one

'So you won your fight!'

Maji swung around. 'See . . . you've done it again!'

'What?'

'Crept up on me!'

'And you've also done it again!'

'What?'

'You're cross again!'

'I'm not!'

'Shhh! Don't talk so loudly. I'm not supposed to be here! I'm supposed to be helping the wives braid their hair.'

'Then why aren't you?'

She shrugged and sat down a little distance from him on the hump of an old termite mound.

He studied her face. 'How do you know I won?'

'I watched.'

'You didn't!'

She looked at him with half-closed eyes. 'I did!'

'You couldn't have. There was no one there except the herders! We fought in the herders' enclosure. Girls aren't allowed inside.'

She sighed and clicked her tongue. 'That doesn't mean I can't watch from outside the enclosure.'

'What do you mean?'

'We watched through the gaps between the poles.'

'You and the wives?'

She clicked her tongue again. 'Tchh! Not the wives. They're too lazy to do anything. I watched with some girls.'

'What?'

She nodded. 'My friends. Ingwe nearly saw me but I hid behind them. They pretended to be sweeping the pathway.'

Then she giggled. 'They call you Boy from the Sea. They think you're strong . . .'

Maji pulled his shoulders back.

'. . . but they say you stick fight in a strange way!'

'What do girls know of stick fighting?'

'That's the problem.'

'What?'

'Girls are never allowed to do exciting things.' She drew squiggles in the sand with her toe.

'What do you want to do?'

'I'd like to be a herder.'

'A herder?'

She nodded. 'Yes. But girls aren't allowed to touch a cow. It's taboo. Herders do as they please. They're free as air. All day long they go where they want. All they do is play reed pipes and follow the sound of cow bells.'

'They work!'

'Hmmph!'

'Mufudzi says it's hard work!'

'What does Mufudzi know?'

'They have to milk the cows.'

'That's easy! I can do that.' She shook her head. 'No . . . boys do what they want to. They're never questioned for being somewhere.'

'And girls? What do girls do?'

She looked straight at him with narrowed eyes as she chewed a stalk of grass. 'You know nothing!' But when she said it, it was not like when Mufudzi was challenging him.

He kept quiet.

'Girls aren't free!'

'Why?'

'They can never do as they please.'

'What do you mean?'

'For girls it's only this long road from a mother's house to the house of a husband's mother.'

'And then?'

'Someone is always telling a girl – Do this! Don't do that! Be quick! Gather these sticks! Hoe this ground! Grind this millet! Mend these fishing baskets! Cook this fish!'

He laughed. 'There're no fishing baskets to mend or fish to cook here. And you don't have to do all those things!'

'What do you mean?'

'You're a promised wife. Promised wives don't have to work. They never have to hoe and plant.'

'No . . . but I have to do what the other wives tell me

to do. I'm never free. I'd like to be a boy so that I can be a herder. Or even a weaver. I'd be happy to sit over a loom and weave all day. But no . . . that job is also only for boys. Only boys may weave cloth for the Mambo.' She jabbed at her drawing with her toe. 'For girls it's just boring things.'

'Then how do you know about fishing baskets and fish?'

'I've fished before.'

'When?'

'I've waded in a river waiting for the fish to be chased towards my basket.' She looked up at him. 'I know about catching fish.'

'Catching fish in a river is easy. Do you know about catching fish in the sea?'

She looked directly back at him. She shook her head but her eyes were dark with mischief. 'So, Boy from the Sea, what else do you know?'

'What?'

She was laughing at him. This he could tell.

'What else do you know, apart from fishing and sticks that speak and a strange way of stick fighting?'

He laughed back at her then. 'I know your name . . . Little Dragonfly!'

Twenty-two

Day after day went by. Many moons had passed since he first arrived in the Kingdom. How many he wasn't sure. Perhaps five?

He walked to all the places where he thought water might be hidden. He gripped the new water-stick tightly. He strained every part of his body as he waited. But the ground remained hard. Indifferent. There was not even a whisper of water seeping between the particles of sand.

The air was white. Dry-white. Sucking at the trees. Sucking at the withered grasses. The sky was as tight as a piece of dry leather pulled across a drum. Things rustled and snapped and creaked and split like the bones of a person too old to stand.

'Mukonikoni . . . Mukonikoni . . . Little Dragonfly . . .' were the only sounds the grass whispered back at him.

He felt tense and hollow with waiting. Waiting for his stick to speak. And waiting to catch a glimpse of her again. Wishing for her suddenly to appear. He walked as close to the wives' enclosure as he dared but still saw no sign of her.

He was beginning to know the faces of the people.

And beginning to know which families belonged to each other and which dogs belonged to which hut. In the middle huts where the families lived, he knew Jee's mother lived. When he passed by he sometimes heard her singing to Jee's baby brother. Across from her hut was the family with five little children who were always squabbling. Behind them lived the woman who kept so many chickens. And across the hard dry ground of the meeting place, the same group of old men sat under the thorns of the big muunga tree.

Now they nodded knowingly when they saw him and some stopped their games of bao and watched as he passed. Women stopped singing and looked up from their hoeing. Girls on the path balancing pots on their heads on their way to the spring searched his face. Mothers weaving stories into their baskets looked up. Old women snaking coils of clay on to pots stopped their work.

A woman smiled as he passed and held out some millet cakes. She didn't speak of the stick. But he knew by the way she smiled and looked, that she was beseeching him to find water.

In the dry stillness everyone seemed to be waiting. It was the season for rain. But rain hadn't come. Not even the Mambo's Rain Dance had brought it.

Now everyone seemed to be expecting something from him. He felt the eyes of the Kingdom on him. Watching. Waiting. But his stick was dead.

Nothing could change it!

Nothing!

Not even Jee demanding, 'When will your stick work? The skins of the cattle hang in folds around their bones. They moan for water.'

Not even Mufudzi challenging, 'My best milk-cow died today! What are you going to do?'

Their challenges filled his ears thicker than wax. But he could do nothing. The stick would not speak! He could not force it to speak. There was nothing he could do. Soon he would have to face the Mambo again. What fate lay ahead for him?

'The Chapungu-men are returning!' Mufudzi announced one afternoon as they reached the red termite mound at their meeting place high on the ridge.

'It can't be!' Maji felt his body stiffen. He tried to recall how many days had passed. But now that his counting stick was broken, he no longer knew. Had the Chapungu-men been gone three moons already? Now the calm would be broken once more.

'They'll come soon. A runner brought a message.' Mufudzi spoke as if the runner had brought the message for him alone.

Jee laughed. 'Then we'll celebrate with dancing and beer and a smile from Mukonikoni for Maji.'

Maji glanced up sharply. 'The return of the Chapungu-men is nothing to celebrate!'

Mufudzi picked up a stone. He hurled it straight at a bright green lizard flashed with red, yellow and blue that was sunning itself on a rock. 'You're right.' Then he looked at Maji. 'In a dry land, water is the only celebration!'

'So?'

'So, at the new moon, the Mambo will dance the Rain Dance again.' He narrowed his eyes. 'Will you find water before then? Will it be a celebration?'

Maji kept silent as he leant against the termite mound. Next to his ear he could hear the restless rustling and scuttling of the termites inside the nest. Yes . . . the return of the Chapungu-men was nothing to celebrate. Bere would influence the Mambo. He was the Mambo's brother! And Bere would make sure he was dealt with.

'The old men say the big muunga tree in the meeting place is dying.' Mufudzi aimed another stone at the lizard.

Jee stopped playing. 'That tree always looks as if it's dying. Then it surprises everyone with green leaves again after the rains come.'

'This time they say it won't! I've scratched it myself. The sap isn't running. The old men say that the tree is the spirit of the Mambo. If it dies, the Mambo dies.'

'The Mambo is not ill! You never have happy news, Mufudzi!'

Mufudzi shrugged. 'They say what they say.' This time his stone hit the lizard.

Later, when Maji got to the muunga tree, he scratched the thick bark with his nail. Mufudzi was right. No sap ran. He rested against the rough trunk and looked out through the twisted, leafless branches. What now? The land shimmered with heat waves. Just like the sea. But the blue sea of Kilwa with its harbour full of dhows and jahazis was far, far away. He would never return. Now his fate was near. Would the Mambo have him killed?

Suddenly, as if from nowhere, Ingwe appeared next to him under the tree.

'Your time has come, Maji.'

'What do you mean?'

'You've been in the Kingdom for nearly six moons now. I have already asked the Mambo five times to give you more time. I cannot ask again. The season of rain has come and gone. None has fallen. The Mambo will dance again at the next new moon. He has given you until then. If you fail, you'll be sent to work at the stone quarries.'

'You mean I will not be killed?'

'Cutting stone for the walls is as good as being dead. Stone workers do not live long. If you want to stay alive, there's no time left. Your stick *must* find water!'

As he spoke the wind began to gust. It lifted swirls of dust. It drew up spirals of grit and brittle leaves into the air. But the stick lay still like a heavy log in Maji's hands. The wind blew fiercer. Dust rose in tight, angry coils and stung his eyes. The sky turned dark and fierce, as if a huge fire burnt somewhere.

They sat close against the tree for shelter. Then Maji asked the question that was burning in him. 'Does the Mambo always marry a wife who has been promised?'

Ingwe looked at him sharply. 'Of course he does,' he hissed.

'Always?'

'Only if a girl shamed herself would the Mambo refuse to marry her.'

'Could a girl refuse to marry the Mambo?'

'Never!'

'What if the girl preferred to marry someone else?'

'It's never considered!' His words had as much anger in them as the wind.

'But if . . .'

'The only time a promised wife may have another husband is when the Mambo dies.'

'If the Mambo dies, do they choose their own husband?'

Ingwe picked up a stone and hurled it against another rock. 'No! They marry the Mambo's brother.'

Maji twisted around to look at him. 'Bere? You mean Bere? Mukonikoni, the Little Dragonfly, will marry Bere?'

Ingwe stood up. 'Yes! By custom, yes!' He turned sharply. 'But you use my sister's name too freely!'

'Your sister?'

'Mukonikoni!' Ingwe glared at him with eyes as stormy as the clouds.

'What?'

'The promised wife is my sister.'

'But—'

'Forget all this nonsense!' Ingwe snapped. 'Forget the promised wife!'

'But . . .' Maji bit his lip.

Ingwe took him by the shoulders and shook him. 'Do you understand? Forget her!'

His words were taken by the wind and flung across the barren ground.

Maji tasted blood on his lip. Now it made sense. On the journey, Ingwe had carried the water-skins. Ingwe had known the route. But Bere had held some sort of power. His words had held some sort of threat.

'Do you understand?' Ingwe demanded again. 'You are here to find water! Now find it!' Then he turned abruptly and walked away.

Maji stared after him. He should have guessed. Mukonikoni had spoken about catching fish and mending fishing baskets. And the drawing in the sand? It had been a fish, not a bird. The people in the Kingdom were not *her* people either. She had grown up on the same island as Ingwe in the middle of the Great River. Her people had been taken by the Mambo. She had been captured and brought here.

Little Dragonfly. One who hovers above water. One who was once free.

The wind suddenly dropped. The storm had passed. But no rain had fallen. The sky pressed down heavy as a thick blanket. The air was quiet again. As quiet as a dead man's heart.

Maji sat hunched against the tree trunk without seeing.

Bere was the Mambo's brother. And Mukonikoni was Ingwe's sister.

Twenty-three

A great cloud of dust filling the sky announced the return of the Chapungu-men. From the termite mound Maji could see them far in the distance, winding between the boulders and trees. They moved in a dark wide stream like an army of ishwa ants on the march. He watched them as he imagined a wounded animal would watch a column of ants approaching. A baboon barked a sharp warning and a troop of tsoko monkeys swung quickly through the thorn trees and scattered away over the rocks.

'Aa-eee! Aa-yah! Aa-eee! Aa-yah!' The chanting echoed from ridge to ridge like the women's hoeing songs. Except now the hoeing songs were silent. The people of the Kingdom had stopped what they were doing. They stood stiffly waiting. Even the children playing in the dust were silenced as their mothers gathered them close.

Maji sensed their unease. It was the same unease that settled on the dhow when they watched heavy clouds roll in across the sea. When they stood waiting with the sail tied. Waiting in silence for the wind that would swoop down and the waves that would rise up around them.

Now the valley was filled with chanting.

'Aa-eee! Aa-yah! Aa-eee! Aa-yah!

Come if you have a fighting spirit, and we will shake it from you.

The skin of a mouse does not choke us.

We have swallowed the elephant's hide whole.

If we are hungry, we feed on the wind.

Where we tread the earth shakes.'

The sun flashed off their gold-barbed spears. Their torches still burned. The dull thud of their feet echoed on the hard ground. Their Chapungu masks were battered and torn. The air was filled with the heat of their bodies. They gave off a stench of sweat.

And something else? The air bristled with it.

To Maji it was a smell of anger. A smell of evil.

In the midst of their heat he was an empty husk. He would catch alight in their flames. Leave behind just a single curl of ash.

Which one was Bere?

It was a night of celebration. It was a night of flame and fire.

An owl swooped low over the meeting place. It settled on the edge of the Tower. A hut caught alight. The flames shot high into the black night. A tree burned like a torch. It showered the air with orange sparks. Ash as soft as sea-foam drifted down against his face.

Flames flickered and spurted. Spluttered on oiled cloths tied to stakes. Dancers swayed beneath them. In the darkness the stakes that held the burning cloths were completely lost. Only the flames could be seen. Like ribbons of fire they wove their own dance above the heads of the dancers under them.

Even the shadows of the thorn trees danced their own spirit dance.

Aa-eee! Aa-yah! Aa-eee! Aaa-yah!

Maji searched the frenzied faces. But he couldn't find her. Not even a glimmer.

Drums vibrated. Feet stamped on hard ground. Eyes reflected red. Sweat beaded on foreheads. Cheeks glistened gold. Heads surrounded by wisps of smoke floated separate from bodies. A stamping mass of people danced through the night and long into the next day. The entire valley was filled with smoke. It rose up and curdled with the clouds until the sun was hidden and the sky was the colour of smouldering grass.

It was then that the horn began calling. Drums beat in the heavy air. The m'bira twanged. The Chapungu-men had returned. Now it was time for the Rain Dance.

This time he knew what to expect. He stood near the women's entrance, hoping to catch a glimpse of her in the procession, while he listened to the words of the praise-singers.

'Lion! Destroyer! One with the deep, rumbling growl.
One who frightens others by the terror of his mane.
One with the deep, rumbling growl.
Crusher of bones, whose eyes are terrible to behold.
One who roams in the dark.
One who has only to roar once.'

His stomach clenched tight. Was he the one to be crushed?

Someone tugged at his shoulder. He heard the soft *shirr shirr* of seed rattles. A voice rasped at his ear.

'Today the Lion will roar! The Crocodile will snap. Its tail will lash through the sky. Its power will be shown. The Crocodile will call the rain. I have seen it in the hakata.'

Maji looked down and saw a foot with six toes.

Then there was sudden silence.

It was as if the earth had taken a deep breath, waiting for the next moment. The sky took on the strange darkness of a purple bruise. The stone walls glowed with coppery light. Then the Mambo appeared in his lion mask and gold casings. He began his slow dance, moving his arms and head and legs, then spinning faster and faster.

The wives began dancing as well. Amongst them was Mukonikoni.

Now she was more beautiful than ever before. Her face shone with brilliance. She caught his look. Her eyes flashed laughter back at him. She bent her body to the earth and swayed with its curve. Drums beat faster. The dance quickened. Her body was as light as a dragonfly's. She danced before the Mambo with her feet hardly touching the ground.

She was the red dragonfly flitting across water.

She was the sharp moonbeam slicing through the night.

She was the spark that crackled from the fire.

She was the flame that leapt into the sky.

She was filled with beauty and power. But it was not beer that made her powerful. It was knowing she was the most beautiful of the women.

And now it was as if everyone knew. They stopped dancing. Fell silent and watched. Yet the faces around her circle of light did not smile. The faces of the older women turned to stone as she danced.

And then . . .? Then even the sky took notice.

It rumbled and groaned. With a crack it split apart. A thousand snakes of silver slithered across its murky surface and reached down to her.

Chanting and drumming melted together. Drums became thunder. Thunder became drums. Everybody danced then. In silver flashes of light they danced, their bodies twisting, stamping, flinging themselves to the sounds. They danced the thunder far down across the plains all the way to the sea. Then they danced it back over the dry land and the stones and the walls. And they danced it up to the clouds again.

Maji felt the first drop of rain against his face. Then one on his arm.

They began to sizzle against the dry earth. Like drops of hot fat in an iron cooking pot. Slowly at first, making puffs of dust as they fell. Then faster and faster. Until there was no sound left but the beating of water against the tight drum of the earth.

Twenty-four

It rained and it rained. It rained until the rocks ran with streams and the plain was a marsh. It rained until the paths between the huts became rivers. It rained until the shrivelled crops with their short, weak roots were washed away. It rained until chickens squatted with drooping wings in the tops of trees and cattle stood up to their knees in water. It rained through the darkness of four days and the blackness of four nights.

For four days Maji, Jee, Mufudzi, Nungu, Tsoko, Tsinza and the other herders rolled and wrestled in the mud between the enclosures. At night they built smoky fires with damp wood in the centre of their hut and they lay on their sleeping mats, smelling the wet earth smells and listening to the water thudding against the grass roof.

And the music of Jee's mutoriro filled the hut with bright, chirping sounds and tickled Maji's heart.

He was light with happiness. He stood in the rain with his arms stretched wide as he had stood in the prow of Tamu's dhow in a storm, feeling the water drench him. The pool of the spring was full. The

Motelekwe was gushing through its rock pools finding its way to the sea. Nothing more would be expected of him. Now he would be allowed to leave. Now he too would find his way to the sea.

And then . . . ? And then the Mambo died.

He died somewhere during those four days when the rain fell. No one could say exactly when. And no one could say exactly why. Not even Mufudzi.

'The N'anga will have to be consulted,' he announced.

'Perhaps he was killed by the lightning bird,' Jee suggested.

'You speak with no sense.' Mufudzi flicked a thick clod of mud into the sky with a stick. 'If the lightning bird killed him, who was the person dancing the Rain Dance after the lightning struck?'

'It's true!' Jee insisted. 'I saw a fire falcon pull the Mambo's spirit from his body. It circled with it three times around the rocks of the Mambo's enclosure before flying off with it into the sky.'

'It was the beer in your head that saw a fire falcon, Jee!'

'It was an owl Jee saw,' Maji reminded them. 'Remember? The night the Chapungu-men returned. It swooped over the meeting place.'

'An owl means death. But whose death?' Jee was looking from one to the other now.

Mufudzi clicked his tongue impatiently. 'The Mambo's, of course!'

'How do you know?'

Mufudzi spoke as if to a small child. 'Remember where the owl sat?'

Jee screwed up his eyes. 'On the rim of the Tower.'

'So . . . ?'

Maji interrupted. 'On the rim with the crocodile-teeth pattern around it.'

'Exactly! And the Tower is . . .'

'The symbol of the Mambo!' Jee said before Mufudzi could get the words out.

Mufudzi looked hard at him. Then he spoke quickly so as not to be interrupted again. 'The owl came with a message of death. To tell it was time for the Chief Crocodile to return to the pool of the spirit world. I knew the owl was telling of the Mambo's death!'

'Then why didn't you speak before?' Jee's voice was full of scorn.

Mufudzi took no notice. 'The Mambo's body is lying waiting. People must come from all over the Kingdom to pay their respect. The body is covered by the skin of a black ox in a hut specially built for his death. It is guarded by the Mambo's eldest sister and the Chapungu-men.'

'How do you know?' Jee asked.

'I know what I know.' Mufudzi flicked his stick so hard through the air that it whistled. 'Don't believe Maji is the only one who has seen inside the Mambo's enclosure. Already the stone-carvers are carving the wood for the falcon that will stand for the Mambo.'

'How can they be carving wood? Stone-carvers carve stone,' Jee argued.

'Hmmph!' Mufudzi snorted. 'That shows how little you know!'

'What then?'

'The falcon is first carved in wood. The elders choose the best carving. Then it's carved in stone. They'll set it in the sacred place with all the other sacred carvings.'

'You think you know everything!' Maji reached out and stopped Mufudzi's stick in midair. Their eyes met.

Mufudzi stared back. 'It's my job to know. A herder must know and see everything! Jee should know too. But Jee spends his time making music instead of listening and seeing.'

Jee looked at him scornfully. 'You are full of big talk and wind, Mufudzi! You make as much noise as an elephant farting after eating too many mupfura fruit! If you're so clever tell us how the Mambo died!'

'That is for you to work out!' He spoke as if he already knew the answer.

'But . . .' Maji bit his lip to try and hold back the question.

'But what?'

'What of Bere?'

'Bere will marry the Mambo's wives.' Mufudzi paused for a moment and looked at Maji. 'And the promised wife. It's our custom. He'll be the new Mambo. And as the new Mambo he'll marry Mukonikoni.'

Twenty-five

Maji saw her again at the ritual sacrifice of the ox made by the Mambo's sister on the huge flat stone next to the women's entrance to the Great Enclosure.

She seemed a stranger. The laughter in her eyes had disappeared. The lightness in her movements had gone. She wore no jewellery. Only a bark string around her neck. Even the moon-shell was gone from her forehead. Like all the other wives, a small patch of her hair had been shaved. But unlike the other wives, she was wearing the black and white striped skin of a zebra around her waist.

'The zebra is the symbol of a girl preparing for marriage,' Mufudzi said with a sly glance at Maji.

Later Jee whispered in his ear. 'Hurry!'

'Why?'

'Mukonikoni.'

'What about her?'

'I've a message from her.'

'What is it?'

'She wants you to come to the cave.'

'What about Ingwe?'

'He's not there. He's training the falcons. No one must see you. Go quickly! Hurry now!'

Maji took care no one was watching as he climbed the path. When he reached the cave, she sat trembling.

'What is it? Are you cold?' He folded one of Ingwe's skin cloaks around her.

'I had a terrible dream.'

'What?'

'Something's going to happen.'

'Sssh! Calm down,' Maji whispered close to her ear.

'But something terrible is going to happen!'

'What? What did you dream?'

'I don't know. I'm scared.'

'Tell me the dream.'

'There was fire everywhere.'

'You dreamt of the Chapungu Ceremony.'

'No! It wasn't a ceremony. People with fire were chasing someone. I couldn't see who it was. There was fire everywhere.' She pulled the cloak tighter and shivered. 'I'm scared.'

'Of what?'

'I don't want to marry Bere!'

'Bere or the Mambo, it's surely the same!'

She shook her head.

'Why not? The Mambo ruled by fire. So will Bere!'

'The Mambo ruled by fire because it was expected of him.'

'And Bere? It's also expected of him. It's all the same, whoever you marry.'

She shook her head again. 'No!'

'Why not?'

'You haven't seen Bere as a Chapungu-man.'

'Yes, I have. At the Chapungu Ceremony.'

'The Chapungu Ceremony is nothing. It's just a dance.'

'So?'

'The Mambo loves dancing.'

'So?'

'The Mambo doesn't march out with fire torches! He's not as fierce as people think. He dances and calls the spirit of rain. But when the Chapungu-men leave the Kingdom and march out, it's no longer a dance.'

'What do you mean?'

'They come with sticks of fire to a village. They're evil. They're far from the Kingdom. It's not a dance any more! It's not even a celebration!'

'What then?'

'They do what they want. They set the huts alight. They kill.' Then softly, softly . . . 'They killed my mother.'

Maji caught his breath. 'Your mother?'

She nodded. 'They said she'd left her cooking fire burning. That she wasn't obedient to the Kingdom. That she needed to be taught a lesson.'

She held her breath then the words came out with a shudder. 'Bere gave the order.'

Maji shivered. Yes, Bere! The one with the heart of a hyena! Bere with his terrifying Chapungu mask. Now he understood his power.

'What about Ingwe?'

'Ingwe was helpless. They tied him up. We were both helpless to save her. He made us watch.'

153

In the dark cave Maji felt the hot smell of Bere's breath against his face. He too was helpless against Bere.

She looked across at him. 'What must I do?'

Yes, what? How could she marry the one who'd murdered her mother? But if she refused to marry Bere? The thought was unbearable.

He reached out and put his arm around her. There was no one to see there wasn't the space of a spear between them. He held her close. He felt her shivering against him. 'Can't you plead with the women of the Kingdom? Surely they will help? Surely they will understand?'

She shook her head. 'They follow the law.'

'But they must know it's impossible for you to marry Bere.'

'Some might know. But they understand the rule of Fire.'

'And your friends?'

'My friends know. They also know the older women make sure the rules of the Kingdom are obeyed.'

'But . . .'

'I have to run away!' she whispered against his shoulder.

'Where to?'

'To the Great River.'

'And when you get there? What then? Your village has been destroyed. Your people are gone.'

She shrugged.

'The Great River's not far enough. Bere will never let you go. He'll find you. He'll send his Chapungu-men after you.'

She gave another shrug. 'What else can I do?'

Yes . . . what? If she ran away, they would find her. If she stayed and refused to marry Bere, she'd be killed.

'You have to go much further than the Great River. Beyond Bere's power.'

'Where? His power stretches everywhere!'

'Far beyond the Kingdom. All the way to the sea.'

'The sea?'

He nodded.

'How?'

'With Ingwe. He knows the way.'

'But—?'

'All three of us will go.'

She looked uncertain. 'It's impossible! The sea is so far!'

'Nothing is impossible.'

He looked away from her. In the shadow would she see the doubt in his face? 'We'll follow the river. Then at the sea we'll travel by boat. In a dhow. We'll return to Kilwa. To my father's house where it's safe,' he whispered.

She grabbed hold of his hands. 'It's a dream!'

'A better dream than your fire dream. Wait. I'll show you. You like drawing pictures. Let me show you a dhow!'

At the back of the cave he took a sharp flat stone. On a smooth place on the rock wall he outlined the great wooden hull. He cut deep into the rock so that the boat showed strongly. Then he drew the tall forward-sloping mast with its three-cornered sail swinging freely from the crossbar. He drew the sail billowing, filled by wind

155

and held taut by ropes. He drew waves curling up around the boat. Lastly he scratched a figure in the prow and two in the stern.

'See! Three of us! That's how we'll travel home.'

'Home . . . ?'

He nodded. 'Home! All the way back to Kilwa. On the monsoon. We'll ride the winds. We'll outwit the currents. We'll reach the safe harbour of Kilwa.'

'How will we find our way?'

'We'll take our route by the stars. We'll measure the height of the Great Star from the edge of the earth. We'll follow the star patterns. In Tamu's house we'll be home. We'll eat fish caught in the sea, cooked in lime and coconut milk.'

She smiled.

'And sweet crab straight from the shell! And side dishes of bananas with curdled milk, saffron, green ginger and grated mango.'

Mukonikoni began to laugh. 'Stop! You're making me hungry!'

'If we're brave enough we can do it.'

'Home!' she sighed.

But first they had to escape Bere. How would he persuade Ingwe to agree?

Twenty-six

A great quietness fell over the valley on the day of preparation for the Mambo's funeral. Even the dogs and children seemed quieter.

At the termite mound Maji sat watching Mufudzi catch newly-hatched flying ants. They crawled out of the damp ground and flew up in clouds of silvery shimmering wings.

The air was clean and thin from the rain. It was so clear, Maji felt he could stretch out his arm and touch the dogs that were snuffling about in the mud in the valley below. He could see the men gathering in silence at the meeting place under the muunga tree.

'When will it be time to join the procession?'

'The preparations take all morning. The Mambo has to be carried to the Motelekwe river.'

'Why?'

'That's where he'll be buried.'

Jee grinned. 'To keep the spirit cool in the wet sand.'

Mufudzi looked annoyed. 'You won't be joking when his angry spirit comes after you, Jee!'

'But why is there such silence?' Maji asked.

Mufudzi trapped a flying ant in his hand. 'When a dead person is buried, quiet is important. Without calm the spirit is troubled. A troubled spirit causes trouble in the Kingdom.'

'What sort of trouble?'

Mufudzi narrowed his eyes. 'Things you don't want to know about.'

Jee laughed. 'That means you don't know!'

'I know what the women are whispering.'

'What?'

But Mufudzi just stared back at them.

Jee shrugged. 'See . . . he knows nothing! For once, Mufudzi has lost his tongue. There's no troubled spirit!'

'That's what you think, Jee!'

Maji looked back at Mufudzi. 'Will the Mambo's spirit finally rest after he's buried?'

'No! It will only rest after Bere has married all the Mambo's wives! And the promised wife!'

The words stung as sharply as if Mufudzi had flung mud clods at him. There was so little time left. He still had to persuade Ingwe.

Jee lay on his back and took out his mutoriro. The sounds came out long and lonely under his fingers. Down below Maji could see the women preparing as well. They were decorating each other in the women's enclosure. Rubbing peanut oil on their bodies until they glistened. Smearing their hair with wild-apple juice. Tying new cloths around their waists. Patting and shaping and smoothing.

He saw her sitting apart from them. She sat quietly.

Still. A little dragonfly resting on a rock. But she had completely lost her dragonfly spirit. It had flown from her. What was she thinking? What did she feel?

He turned to Mufudzi and Jee. 'What if Mukonikoni doesn't want to marry Bere?'

Mufudzi glanced at him as if he had asked something very stupid. Then he went on scooping up flying ants. Jee stopped playing and stared at the clouds. Neither of them answered. Every time Mufudzi caught an ant, he pulled off each wing individually and slipped the fat, wriggling body into his mouth.

'You haven't answered!'

Mufudzi shrugged. 'It can't happen. She has to!'

'But what if?'

Mufudzi sucked his teeth noisily with his tongue.

Maji felt like hitting him. 'Stop that!'

'What's the matter? You're as angry as a wasp!'

'Nothing!'

A horn called. Long and drawn out. Then a procession emerged from the entrance of the Mambo's enclosure on the opposite ridge.

The air was so still, he could hear the grunts of the men as they struggled over the loose boulders. They were carrying the Mambo's body on a stretcher covered by a white cloth. The Chapungu-men followed with the gold ceremonial spears. He squinted into the sunlight. Which of them was Bere?

Mufudzi stood up. 'Come! It's time to join them.'

Maji and Jee followed in silence along the path. As they got closer people began gathering from all sides.

The Chapungu-men were joined by the women's procession. Then the bearers stopped. They turned in a circle. First one way then the other, while the women chanted and clapped.

He glanced at Mufudzi. 'What's that for?'

'To muddle the spirit. So the Mambo's spirit won't find its way back to the valley before he's at rest.'

Then the crowd surged forward. Up ahead he saw Bere. He was wearing his cloak of animal tails that twisted and swung and trailed on the ground as he moved. In his hands he held three of the finely cut gold spearheads. Around his neck he wore the necklace of turtle shell.

It was too late for Maji to turn away. Bere's eyes had challenged him. The far corners of the sky and the plains seemed to grow dark. Next to him he heard the N'anga's raspy voice. 'The old Crocodile is dead! The new Crocodile's teeth will snap. Its tail will lash. It will show its power.'

And in the distance he saw a girl dressed in zebra skins.

PART SEVEN
FIRE

Twenty-seven

Day after day the air vibrated with the twanging of m'biras. The sound seeped into every crevice. Filled every pathway. Echoed through every rock. There was no end to it. No escape. It flowed behind Maji like a shadow at his back, which no amount of shrugging could shake off. The m'biras were calling the ancestral spirits.

The women began preparing for the wedding. And Ingwe began collecting poison herbs.

'Herbs? What for?'

'To sprinkle in the cave. To keep mites away from the falcons.'

Maji narrowed his eyes against the sun and studied Ingwe's face. Was he telling the truth? Would someone be mixing poisons at the time of a wedding?

Above them the falcons circled slowly and made shadows on the ground as they flew against the sun. The dark shapes reminded him of the Chapungu-men and Bere. He watched Ingwe grinding the herbs in a hollow stone. Who was he pounding the poisons for? Was he planning something more serious than poisoning the falcon mites? Now was the time to speak.

'Do you have a plan?'

'A plan?' Ingwe looked up. 'What do you mean . . . a plan?'

'To help.' He swallowed hard. Ingwe had warned him not to use her name. 'To help Mukonikoni. She wears the zebra skin.'

'So?'

'In preparation for marriage.'

'Do you think I haven't seen what skin she wears?' Ingwe went on pounding.

'We must escape. It's our only chance.'

'*We* must escape? *WE?*'

Maji nodded.

'And where do you think *WE* must go?'

'Back to the sea.'

'The sea?' Ingwe stared back at him with dark eyes.

'You know the way.'

'There are many of them and only three of us. We wouldn't get far.'

'We could slip away without them realizing. We could get a few days ahead of them.'

'Don't be a fool! Do you think we could just disappear?' He snapped his fingers. 'Just like that! Do you think it'd go unnoticed that the promised wife had disappeared?'

Maji kept silent.

'And even if we managed, what would we do once we reached the sea? Bere knows his way there as well. He could follow us if he wanted to. Remember what I said. Bere is the hyena. He doesn't stop until every last bone is crushed.'

'We could outwit him.'

'How?'

'At the sea we could build a dhow. Take the monsoon winds. Sail north. Far out of Bere's reach.'

'Tch! You speak as if the journey to the sea and building a dhow is as easy as plucking these herbs off a bush! Have you forgotten? Don't you remember how hard the journey was? How we thirsted for water? How the sun beat down?'

Maji drew himself up straighter. 'I was a boy then.'

'And now?'

'I'm a man!'

Ingwe went on pounding.

'We should try.'

Still he was silent.

'For Mukonikoni's sake!'

Ingwe glanced up sharply. 'Who are you to name her so freely? I'm her brother. Do you think I want her to marry Bere? Do you think I don't have a plan?'

'Yes, but what?'

Ingwe's eyes silenced him. 'It's not for you to know!'

Twenty-eight

The marriage preparations went on. Now there was great energy. The walls of the huts were painted with patterns of red ochre and white clay. The floors were polished with fresh dung. The roofs were given new thatch. Each chore had its own special song. A song for making patterns. A song for polishing. A song for thatching. And the girls smiled at Maji as he passed.

Then it was time to make the marriage beer. The millet brought by people from all over the Kingdom to honour the Mambo's death was collected and the women began making huge pots to hold the special beer. First they knelt. Then they stood to add the last thick snakes of clay to the tall pots. They polished the pots with river pebbles, then left them standing in rows to dry pale in the hot sun.

When it was time for the pot firing, Maji and Jee and Mufudzi helped dig the huge pit. The pots were carried carefully and arranged on their sides in the hollow. Dried grass, tree bark, leaves and dried cow-dung were packed around them according to the older women's instructions. They sat at a distance from the heat pinching snuff to their noses and giving orders.

'Take care! The burning ashes must fall into the pots.'

'Now scatter a mound of the same mixture on top!'

'Do not pack it too tightly. The fire will smother! It needs air.'

Then the grass under the pots was lit by the younger women. Thick, coppery smoke rose up into the sky. The air was filled with heat and confusion.

'Careful! Let air reach the ashes.'

'It's burning too fast. Throw on damp leaves. The pots will crack!'

'It's burning too slow. The pots won't be strong enough. Loosen the heap!'

'Pile on more leaves!'

'Take them off! It's too much!'

'Mufudzi! Jee! Fetch more cow-dung!'

In all this, the older women were the important ones. They were the ones who had to be obeyed. The pots that held beer for a Mambo's wedding had to be perfect.

Words of a song wove through the smoky air as they worked.

'We have taken your old name from you.

You are now called Mambo of the people.

You judge and you punish.

You are a knife that cuts evenly on every side.'

Despite the heat of the fire and the sweat on his skin, Maji shivered as he heard the words. It was Bere who was the new Mambo. Bere who would judge and punish.

Far away he heard the plucking sound of a m'bira. Where were the ancestral spirits of the Kingdom now? And where were his ancestral spirits?

When Mufudzi and Jee came back with a basket of cow-dung, their mouths were full of strange talk.

'She's gone,' Mufudzi announced.

'Who?'

'The Mambo's wife.'

'The Mambo has many wives.'

'The Mambo's promised wife.'

'Mukonikoni? Is it true?'

Mufudzi nodded.

Why would she have gone without telling him? He thought of the poison. Who was it for? Would Ingwe poison his own sister because he didn't want her to marry Bere? No, surely not. Perhaps he was hiding her.

'We must find Ingwe.'

'Ingwe has disappeared as well.'

Maji stared at Mufudzi. 'What?' Would they both have gone without him?

'She's a wild one,' one of the older women said as she piled more dung on the heap.

'She needs discipline!' another woman said, poking at the fire.

'Her mother should've taught her better ways.'

'What can you expect of river people? They know no better.'

'But she's young!' A woman glanced around the circle as if to silence them with her eyes. 'You can't blame her! She came to the Kingdom without a mother!'

'No matter! She still needs discipline!'

'She was the Mambo's favourite.'

'Tch! The Mambo should not make a woman from another tribe his favourite!'

'She's Bere's favourite too. Bere will find her.'

'She has spurned him.'

'Bere will punish her.'

'She must be punished!'

'But I tell you . . . she's young! You can't blame her! She came here without a mother!'

'Tchh! You forget! Remember the night of the Rain Dance? The night the Mambo died? She danced as if *she* were calling the rain!'

'No! That's not true! She was dancing like any young girl at a celebration!'

'No! *She* called the rain!'

'That's isn't true!'

'She has no right to call the rain!'

'Only the Mambo has the right to call rain.'

'She practises uroyi!'

There was a sharp intake of breath.

'Uroyi? Uroyi! Uroyi!' was passed like a hot coal from mouth to mouth.

'Stop! It's not true! She's only a girl!'

'She must be found!'

'Perhaps she's hiding in Ingwe's cave.'

'The N'anga will know where to find her.'

'The N'anga knows what must be done if there's uroyi.'

The older women left off their snuff taking. The pot-fires were left to smoulder. Everyone seemed to be running one way or another. Chickens scattered. Dogs barked.

Maji caught the eyes of a few women who remained standing. One of them was the woman who had argued against the others. Another was Jee's mother. Now she looked straight back at him. Then she shook her head and turned and walked slowly away. The others followed quietly behind her.

'What is it? What's happening?'

Jee shrugged. 'Take no notice. It's women's talk.'

'They speak of uroyi!' Mufudzi answered.

Maji swung around to face him. 'Uroyi?'

'Witchcraft!'

'But why?'

'They say she called the rain. That she danced the Rain Dance. They say she's a witch!'

'They can't believe that!' He pointed behind him. 'You saw the woman who stood here. You heard what she said. She doesn't believe it. And you saw Jee's mother. And you saw her shake her head. There must be others who don't believe as well but are too scared to speak out.'

'It's what *most* believe!'

'So?'

'They say she must be found.'

'And when she's found?'

Jee and Mufudzi were silent. Overhead thunder rolled around the ridge and between the rocks. The heavy clouds pressed down on him.

'It would be better if she weren't found.' Jee spoke quietly. 'If they find her . . .'

'Yes?'

'If they find her, she'll be burnt.' Mufudzi spoke the words as if there were no doubt.

'What?'

Neither Mufudzi nor Jee spoke.

'Why? How can you be so sure?'

Mufudzi looked at him. 'The old women say she's a witch. Muroyi, muroyi, is what they're whispering! I've heard the stories they stir into their cooking pots.'

'What stories?'

'They say the owl that sat on the rim of the Tower was Mukonikoni's spirit. They say *she* was the one who brought death to the Mambo. They say she danced like someone possessed on the night of the Rain Dance. She practised uroyi! And a witch must be killed. Remember, the Mambo rules by fire!'

Maji grabbed Mufudzi by the shoulders and shook him. 'They say! *They* say! That's all *you* ever say! But do you *know*?'

Mufudzi glared back at him.

'No! You see! You don't!' Maji shoved him away. 'No one knows! How can anyone be so foolish as to think Mukonikoni is a witch?'

Mufudzi's eyes slid scornfully over him. 'Remember the dragonfly is not always beautiful. The dragonfly starts life like an anti-lion!'

'So?'

Jee stood up and pushed between them. 'Maji's right!

171

Mukonikoni's not a witch. You heard that woman speak. She danced as any young girl dances.'

Mufudzi looked hard at them. 'Were both your fathers monkeys? Can't you see?'

'What?'

'She bewitched the Mambo. She has bewitched Bere. She has even bewitched the two of you!'

'That's not true!'

'She bewitches everyone with her beauty. She catches people like an ant-lion catches ants in her claws! The old women know. They don't like it. No one should have such power! Their anger is great. She is a muroyi, they say. And witches must be burned!'

As he stopped speaking, a wild streak of lightning flashed across the horizon and split the dark sky with a crack. They rushed into a rock crevice for shelter.

'See! The dead Mambo's spirit is speaking!' Mufudzi shouted. 'He's angered. His lightning falcon is pouncing. It's searching for Mukonikoni! Ready to strike her!'

'Don't listen to him,' Jee whispered close to Maji's ear. 'The lightning falcon is a good thing. It won't strike Mukonikoni. It'll light up the dark places so we can find her. Don't worry. She'll be safe.'

But above the noise of the thunder Maji was listening to another sound. This time it was not the m'biras. It was a sound as restless as termites rustling in a nest.

The sound of wind rushing through reeds.

The sound of flames crackling.

Feet thudding. Drums beating.

He heard it echo in the rock next to his ear. He

172

felt it shiver through the soles of his feet. They had already lit the torches from the smouldering pot-fire. The women's anger was great. And Bere's power was great. He felt it gathering. Mufudzi was right. A few voices speaking out were not enough. The women who had taken their children and hidden away in their huts could no longer help.

Now he could smell the anger. The stench of evil stung his nostrils.

He heard the voices. 'Muroyi! Muroyi!'

He turned to Jee. In his eyes he saw fear.

Then he heard the cry again. 'Muroyi! Muroyi! She must be burned!'

Along pathways, between huts, around rocks, alongside stone walls, came a great moving mass of flame. But the flames were not moving out of the Kingdom, carried by the Chapungu-men but moving inwards to the meeting place, carried by the women.

Aa-eee! Aa-yah! Aa-eee! Aa-yah!

A river of flame swung between the rocks, as angry as a crocodile's tail. A creature of fire. A monster that slithered over the rocks, its nostrils snorting tendrils of flame, its tail whipping fire as it climbed upwards towards Ingwe's cave.

Aa-eee! Aa-yah! Aa-eee! Aa-yah!

The cave! That's where she was. That's where they were going! He pushed past Jee and Mufudzi into the path of the flame-carrying beast.

It surged forward, gathering others along the way. Now Maji was caught up in the stomach of its chant.

173

Aa-eee! Aa-yah! Aa-eee! Aa-yah!

Flames fanned out around him. Smoke stung his eyes.

He fought to get ahead of the writhing fire-beast. Paths too narrow couldn't hold it back. It spread out over rocks. Leapt across chasms. Dry grass and twigs caught alight as it passed. He felt the heat of its flame-hot breath lick his face. He smelt the evil hate-smell of its body.

Then he heard its cry up ahead. Full of victory. Muroyi! Muroyi!

He was too late! Through the thick smoke dark shapes were outlined against the glow. They were already at the cave. He saw them throw down torches at the entrance. They fed the fire with sticks and bushes. He heard the crackle as branches caught. A great wall of flame shot upwards. So fierce that those in front leapt back.

He squinted into the white heat. But no figure appeared at the entrance.

Flames licked the boulders and plaited high into the air, sending explosions of sparks upwards. Every brittle tree, every blade of grass was alight. The whole rock face was on fire.

Suddenly a crack like thunder rang out as shards of rock split and shattered and fell from the boulders.

He stood transfixed.

Then the first raindrops fell. At first delicate like ash against his face. Then they beat down in a solid mass against his body until he was drenched. Everything was lost in a smouldering grey haze of smoke and rain. Flames withered away. Torches went out.

But deep inside the cave, beyond the reach of the downpour, a raging inferno still burned. He saw the outline of people against it. People standing in silence in the beating rain, waiting for the fire inside to subside. They stood with their arms slack at their sides. Their fury spent. All strength drained. Waiting to see what the ashes of the cave would finally reveal.

Maji could not stand still. He could not wait. He wanted to be gone from that place. He wanted to run. He turned and stumbled down the path through the rain without any sense of knowing where he was going or where he wanted to go. Lightning pounced from all directions. In sudden flashes, the stone walls rose up in every detail. The jagged hyena jaw of the ridge tore at the sky. It was hunting him. Watching and waiting for the moment to strike. To crunch down and carry him off.

He had been stupid to believe his power would help him. To think he could escape Bere. The N'anga had seen his fate in the hakata. The Crocodile and the Snake had made patterns. And the N'anga had known the Crocodile would win.

He should have known too.

The Spirit of Fire had overcome the Spirit of Water.

Twenty-nine

Rain beat against his face. Blinded him. Something reached out and gripped his arm. He shook himself free. He would not stop for this creature.

'Maji!'

It was Jee. He pulled Maji under an overhang of rock. Around them the rain fell as solid as a sheet of silver.

'You must leave the Kingdom. You must go!' Jee shouted above the sound of the rain.

'Where?'

'To the Motelekwe.'

'Why?'

'Escape before it's too late! There's no time left!'

'But—?'

'Just believe me. You must hurry! There's too much to explain. But not now! There's no time! You must go!'

Maji grabbed hold of his arm. 'Come with me, Jee!'

Jee shook his head. 'I can't.'

'Why?'

'This is my place. It's the place of my mother and my father.'

'You can have a new home!'

'No . . . this is where I belong. My ancestors are here. My spirit belongs here.'

'But you've seen the power of fire. You've seen the anger!'

'I'm not afraid. No. This is my home. It's not good to go too far from your home. Then you forget who you are.' He pushed something into Maji's hands. 'Take this for your journey. These gifts will keep you strong. Now you must leave. Go well my friend!'

'I can't leave without knowing. Is Mukonikoni alive? Where is Ingwe? What of Bere?'

'There's no time to tell everything! But she's safe!' Jee held him by the shoulders for a moment then he pushed him off impatiently. 'Now go while there's still confusion.'

'But—?'

Jee shoved against his chest. 'Go! Go . . . I say!' Then he stepped backwards into the rain. It fell like a cloak of silver around his face and shoulders. 'I see you, Maji. I am well if you are well, my brother.'

Then he was gone.

Maji stood staring after him. 'Jee . . . come back!' But there was no reply. He'd disappeared. 'Haya kwa heri! Haya kwa heri!' The words tumbled out and were lost in the roar of the rain.

In his hands he held the fighting stick Jee had carved for him and two stitched skin pouches and a thin reed with holes in it. It was Jee's mutoriro.

Then he began running.

Boulders streamed with water. Paths flowed like rivers.

At the red termite mound on the ridge, he stopped briefly to catch his breath. He looked back. The fire inside the cave still burned with a fierce glow. But the rain had eased off. He could see the torches being lit again. Far in the distance against a strange coppery glow, he saw six dark specks. It was the falcons. They flew higher and higher, climbing their own spirals into the sky. Soon they were lost.

Then suddenly around a bend in the path, there was a figure. It was Ingwe.

Maji sucked in his breath, almost too afraid to ask. 'Mukonikoni? Is she . . .?'

'No!' Ingwe shook his head. 'She's safe. I sent her away in time. She's ahead of us. We must hurry. Before the Chapungu-men realize her body's not in the cave. She's waiting at the river.'

Under them the ground was slippery. The rain had stopped. But mud sucked at their feet. Mist dragged at their bodies. Across the mountains, a sharp thin moon caught at the clouds. Maji felt he was moving in a dream.

Suddenly up ahead he heard the roaring water. The Motelekwe was a raging torrent. It swept past, pulling trees with it, flowing full and strong, bulging up over rocks, swirling around boulders too large to swallow.

There was a shimmer. Out of the corner of his eye, he saw something white. A torn piece of zebra skin caught on a branch.

Maji ran forward. Mukonikoni? Had the river taken her? His eyes darted downstream. In the dim light he saw her clinging to a rock with water heaving past on either side of her. Trapped by the force of it.

'Quick!' Ingwe shouted above the roar. 'Find a branch for her to grab. We'll pull her to the bank.'

'The current's too strong. She won't have enough strength to hold on. She'll be swept away.'

His eyes rushed back to Mukonikoni. Already the water had risen to around her shoulders. 'There's no time left. I must swim to her!'

He threw down Jee's gifts.

Ingwe grabbed him. 'Don't be a fool, Maji! That's not the way to save her. You'll both be swept away. All the way to the sea!'

'Isn't that what you said? That I belong to the sea?'

'Yes, but not like this! Not now!'

'But what if the sea knows me? What if the sea comes up the river to fetch me and carries me back to the coast? What if the sea holds no fear for me . . . as long as she is saved?'

'Then you must go!'

Maji sucked in his breath, then jumped.

The air was punched from his body as he hit the water. The current took hold of him. It swept him along as lightly as a piece of driftwood. He was drawn under, but came up again as he was whirled into a deep basin. He clutched along the rocks. Fingers clawed for grooves that weren't there. He sucked at air before being pushed under again. This was a force he couldn't fight. It was taking him. Taking him. Everything had disappeared. His head was singing. There was nothing. Just darkness.

Then suddenly his head was above the water again. She was there in front of him. Her eyes wide and terrified above the bulging water.

He stretched his arm out and grabbed. Graceful dancer, I offer you the spirits of my ancestors. I am your turtle. He gripped her tightly. Then the water took them both. It pulled and dragged at their bodies. It swept them on towards a bend. Maji felt her slipping from his grip. He was losing her.

Suddenly there was a shape up ahead. It was Ingwe crouched on a rock in the middle of the river. He was shouting but the roar of the water drowned his voice. He stretched towards them. Maji felt Mukonikoni being dragged from his arms. But it was too late for him. The force of the water swept him past Ingwe. Nothing would help now. It was too late. His arms had no strength left. He was numb and powerless. Caught up in the churning stomach of the river. It had sucked him in and was refusing to vomit him out again.

Ingwe was right. It would take his spirit and spew it out only when it reached the sea. He was returning to Tamu. This is how Ingwe said it would be.

He was drawn deeper and deeper into the stomach of the raging beast. Now there was only darkness around him. The water boiled and churned and held him as surely as the tentacles of an octopus.

He heard its voice. Don't trust me! Don't trust me! I'm warning you! Don't trust me! Don't blame me for my whirlpools and undertows. Don't blame me for wanting to devour you.

Where were the turtles to save him now? Was the mark on his leg in the shape of a turtle all for nothing?

Voices call him.

Arms reach out for him. Hands touch him. Pull him along to a place far from the sun. Far, far away.

He descends into the dark.

Come! Come with us . . . the voices sing.

There is darkness and howling. Water lashing. A sail ripping. Wood wrenching. Snapping.

A spiral of darkness.

He weaves through it.

A light comes towards him. He reaches out for it.

It shatters into myriads of colours.

Jewels as bright as any he has ever seen. Glass beads.

They explode around him. Colours fill his head. More magical than any Persian carpet.

No! No! Not yet! It's *not* time! It's not time! He tries to pull away from the hands that draw him along. From the voices that fill his head. It's not Tamu calling him! These are not Tamu's arms guiding him.

Now he knows. He cannot go. The sea cannot claim him. Not yet! He's not ready to be claimed.

He begins to claw his way back. To pull free from the beast that wants to devour him. With a powerful thrust, he breaks free from its grip and reaches towards the light.

He gasps air.

There's a shape of something dark ahead. A turtle? Can it be?

No. It's a tree. Wedged between two giant boulders. This is his only chance. His body is hurled into it. He stretches out. Grabs. He locks his arms around the rough bark. He feels his legs being swept along under him. Not now. Not now. He refuses to let go. Refuses to give himself back to the sea. With all the strength left in him, he holds on.

PART EIGHT
FIRE AND WATER

Thirty

He lies for a long time waiting for his body to come alive. He hears the sound of water. It must be the sea. Yes, he is lying on the sand next to Tamu.

A memory stirs in him. Far, far away. What?

He dips into the memory. A long journey through dry land. A leopard-cloaked man. A Kingdom of Stone. A terrifying bird. A girl dancing as light as a dragonfly. A fire? Water?

What? He tries to catch the memory. But it's like looking deep into the sea on a still day. Far down there are fish shapes. They swim closer to the surface. There are patterns. Colour. Quietly you slip your hand into the water to catch one. But a breeze ruffles the water. The shapes dart away.

Now the memory darts away as well.

Perhaps it's part of a dream. Something he has imagined. Perhaps it's all been a dream. Perhaps the whole story has passed through his imagination in one quick flash. Perhaps there has been no Kingdom of Stone. No fire. No flood.

Perhaps all along he has been lying here on the

sand next to Tamu . . . dreaming.

The turtles are imagined. There are no turtles. None have saved him. Wave after wave has pounded the dhow over the coral. He has been hurled up on the sand next to Tamu. All else has been dreamt. Yes, just a dream . . . a dream fed by the fiery sun and a body burning for a sip of water. All this time he has been lying next to Tamu, dreaming, and waiting to die.

Now here he lies this very instant . . . his body limp and lifeless as a piece of washed-up seaweed. And at this very moment he is giving up his spirit alongside Tamu.

Everything else, the journey, the Kingdom, the fire, has been a dream.

Something white drifts towards him. The dhow's sail? No that is long gone.

The sun? No, not the sun. It's a large white moon.

It can't be. The moon is thin and sharp. Now he remembers. He saw it in the sky as he ran with Ingwe.

Ingwe! Yes, that's his name. Ingwe! The man with the leopard cloak. The man in his dream.

Yet now this is a round moon. It floats towards him. A circle of light, right in front of his eyes. He feels its silvery light covering him like a blanket.

'Maji . . .' the voice of the moon calls. 'Maji . . .'

How does the moon know his name?

The breath of the moon floats against his face. He feels its warmth. How can it be so warm? Is moonbreath not cold?

He breathes in the warm scent of the moon. Then he feels it brush against his mouth. A touch as light as a feather. As soft as the flutter of a wing. A whisper of warmth against his lips. A moonbeam.

'He breathes . . .' the voice of the moon sighs.

He senses the warmth of the moon drift away.

Moonbreath, Moonbreath . . . come back! But his voice has no power.

He opens his eyes wide so that he can command the moon to return.

Above him a face drifts in the pale light.

Now he feels the blood throbbing at his temple. He hears the sound of water rushing by. He remembers something else. Being pulled. Not by waves but by a river. Underneath his body he senses a hard surface. Not sand. But rock. He is lying on a rock.

'He breathes!'

The words drag at his eyelids. He opens them again. The face is still leaning over him.

'What . . . ?'

'Yes . . . ?'

'The moon . . . ? Where has the moon gone to?'

'What moon, Maji?'

A girl's face floats above him. Tied to her forehead is a flat round shell. A moon-shell. Its whiteness reflects silvery stars.

'The moon-shell on your forehead . . . I thought . . .'

'Yes?'

'I thought . . .'

'Yes?'

He feels foolish to admit he thought it was the real moon. 'The moon–shell is not lost . . .' is all he can think to say.

He hears a man's voice next to him. 'No, the moon–shell is not lost. And neither is she. The ancestors of the Great River were calling. But it wasn't time. Your ancestors were calling you as well. But it wasn't time for either of you to leave.'

The girl smiles down at him. Against the pale sky, the real moon with thin horns pointing upwards rests on her head like a silver headdress. Perhaps this is still a dream.

He closes his eyes. 'I'm tired. I need to sleep.'

The moonbreath comes close to him again.

'No Maji!' It whispers near his ear. 'You must wake up! We have far to go!'

He opens his eyes again. 'What . . . ?'

'There's no time to sleep.'

'Is it you . . . ?'

'Who?'

'Little Dragonfly?'

She takes his hand and smiles. 'Who else? You saved me, Maji. The path was washed away. I slipped on a rock. The river was strong. But you came for me.'

He hears the man's voice again. He turns his head. He sees a leopard cloak. It's Ingwe. 'The Motelekwe was fierce. But you fought it well. Like you fought the Kapsuku rapids.'

He closes his eyes and feels the hands pulling him again. Far, far towards the darkness. The voices in his head calling, calling.

'I felt the river take me.'

'But you fought! True to the spirit of your ancestors!'

'My ancestors!' Suddenly Maji was awake. He opened his eyes wide. His water-stick? He felt at his wristband. But it was gone. Lost somewhere in the river. He sat up. He caught Ingwe's look.

'I told you. The power is not in the stick! The power is in you!'

Maji shivered. Now he remembered. Twice in a very short time, the power had nearly gone from him. At the cave, if Bere had come towards him with a torch of fire, his spirit would have gone. He wouldn't have been able to fight. Nothing but an empty husk would've been left behind. Then too in the river when he'd felt the water taking his spirit. Pulling it along, sucking it from him and drawing him into the darkness. Then nothing would've been left but a shell as empty as those of the turtles.

Fire and water had both tested him.

'I have fetched the things Jee gave you.' Ingwe's voice interrupted the pictures in his head.

'What things?'

'His gifts. The fighting stick and the pouches. Like a true herder preparing for a journey, Jee has filled the pouches with sweet potato and wrapped millet cakes for us to take.'

Mukonikoni laughed. 'Good. I'm hungry!'

'There was another gift?'

Ingwe nodded. 'His mutoriro . . . yes.'

'How will he play without it?'

189

'Don't you *yet* understand?'

'What?'

'The music is in him. It's not in the reed.'

Maji smiled as he caught Ingwe's look. Yes, the music was in Jee. He thought of Jee's words – it's not good to go too far from your home. Then you forget who you are – Jee would never forget who he was. He didn't need his mutoriro, or even his fighting stick, to know who he was. Jee was strong and brave. He would survive.

'I have a gift for you as well.' Ingwe pressed something into his hand.

Maji looked down. In the dim light he saw a flash of orange and blue. Cornelian stone lay clasped against lapis lazuli. 'Tamu's ring?'

Ingwe nodded. 'Yours now! Put it on!'

Maji slipped it over his right forefinger. It was too tight for his thumb now.

'I took it from the Mambo's body before the burial ceremony. Without anyone knowing. Your father would've have wanted you to have it.'

He rubbed the silver that had worn so smooth from the sail ropes passing through Tamu's hands. He traced around the collar holding the two stones so tightly together.

Ingwe watched him.

'What is their mystery?' Maji asked.

'What do you think?'

'Tamu said they're symbols of fire and water.'

Ingwe nodded.

'They can't be.'

'Why not?'

'Fire and water are enemies. How can they lie so close together?'

'They exist side by side. They don't have to be enemies. They're equal.'

Maji looked at him. 'Equal? Impossible!'

'No,' Ingwe shook his head. 'Fire has power to dry up water. Water has power to put out fire.'

'But fire destroys.' Maji interrupted. The image of the creature of fire slithering over the rocks came back to him. It was too hard to let go of. 'The Chapungu-men with their torches are destroyers!'

'Water destroys too.' Mukonikoni shivered. 'Today we both nearly drowned.'

For a moment Maji was silent. Yes, he had heard the voice of the water. Don't trust me! Don't trust me. 'Neither fire nor water can be trusted.'

Ingwe shook his head. 'Both are dangerous. But they don't always destroy. Fire cleanses the earth. It gives warmth. Water isn't always like this river. It cools. It brings new growth. Both have power to destroy. Both have power to do good. They exist side by side, each with their own good.'

Maji chewed his lip. 'So they're equal in Tamu's ring – is that their mystery?'

'Exactly!' Ingwe nodded and stood up. 'Now you have rested long enough. We must hurry. We still have enemies. The Chapungu-men will come after us.'

Mukonikoni shuddered and hugged her arms against

herself. Maji saw she was no longer wearing the zebra skin. She had a wrap of cloth and a blanket of skin tied at her shoulders. Ingwe must've given it to her.

'What of Bere?' she asked. 'He'll follow us.'

'No, Bere will not come with them. By custom it's not fit for the Mambo to travel with the Chapungu-men. I know the way better than any of them. Soon it will be completely dark. In darkness we can get far.'

'The Chapungu-men frighten me!' She shuddered again.

'The further we travel, the more we'll shake off our fear of the Chapungu-men.'

'But what of other dangers?'

'If we talk loudly enough, we'll frighten the leopard and lion that hunt at night.'

Maji bit hard against his tongue. It was not as easy as that. He thought of the dry land shimmering endlessly like the ocean, where the scorpion lurked and the cobra coiled. He remembered the darkness beyond the musimbiti trees. He thought of the crocodile head dangling from the creeper. The sharp bite of the crocodile hunters' poison. And the thirst.

Most of all he remembered the thirst.

Mukonikoni knew none of these things. But now was not the time to tell her. Now was not the time to speak of dangers. He caught Ingwe's eye. 'It's a long journey to the sea!' was all he said.

'And the dangers?' Mukonikoni insisted.

'It's a long journey. And all journeys hold dangers. But at the start of a new journey there's always hope!'

192

'Hope? Are you sure?' She looked from one to the other.

Ingwe nodded. 'Keep your eyes clear. Keep watching and you'll be safe. Now we must hurry.' He bent down. 'But first you need to bind this leather around your feet. The path along the way is rough. The thorns sharp.'

'And when we get to the sea?' She began twisting the leather pieces under her soles and around her ankles.

'We'll follow the spirit of Maji's ancestors. At the sea we'll be truly free. The traders at Sofala will help us.'

Maji nodded. 'We'll build a dhow.'

Her dark eyes flashed. 'Have you built one before?'

He shook his head.

'Then how will you know?'

He clicked his tongue. 'I've watched how the planks are cut. I know the wood to use. I know how to tie them with palm fronds. How to caulk the holes with resin and coconut fibre. I know how to choose the timber for the curve of the foremost stem. I know what's needed for a mast to be strong.'

Ingwe laughed. 'It'll have to be a dhow stronger than the one you scratched on the cave wall!'

Mukonikoni glanced up sharply. 'You found the drawing? You knew what Maji was planning?'

'Yes.'

'If the Chapungu–men see it they'll know as well.'

Ingwe shook his head. 'They won't find it. It'll be blackened with soot. We'll be far by then.'

'When the dhow is built, what then?'

Maji clicked his tongue again. 'I will sail as I've always sailed.'

'But by what charts?'

Was she teasing him? He pulled his shoulders back. 'I don't need charts. The charts are in my head. I told you. We'll sail by the stars. By the measurement of the Great Star from the earth's edge. I know the pattern of the stars. And I know the currents. I know where the water flows fastest and the wind blows fiercest.'

He felt for the ring and rubbed the silver that had worn smooth against the sail ropes on Tamu's finger. Now it would feel the bite of the rope again. 'The sea holds no fear for me.'

Ingwe turned as if he had just remembered something. He held out a piece of folded skin. 'Here, wrap yourself in this, Maji.'

When he looked down he saw a pattern of dark patches against pale fur.

'A leopard skin?'

'Put it on! The journey is long and cold.' Ingwe turned away as if to hide his smile.

'What? Why're you smiling?'

Ingwe looked back at him. 'Didn't you say you're a man now? If that is so, it's time you wore a man's cloak.' Then he stood up and walked to the river's edge. When he came back he was holding something.

Maji looked down expecting to see Jee's pouches. But in his hand Ingwe held out two water-skins. 'Take them.'

Maji felt the slippery skin of the wet leather. He heard

the water moving against the sides. For a moment he was puzzled. Then he caught Ingwe's look.

In the silence that was between them, he understood.

On this journey he was to be the waterbearer.

Ingwe smiled. 'Are you ready?'

The Scroll and the Ring

The wave that struck her grandfather had been of gigantic proportions.

In the latticed courtyard of his home, the girl hangs three lamps in the pomegranate tree. Then she sits down on the cool stone steps and pours orange-flavoured water from a flask of thick blue glass. The evening air hums with the sound of bees. A smell of sandalwood and resin wafts on the breeze. Moths drift into the courtyard and flutter between the lamps and the red globules of fruit hanging on the pomegranate tree.

From the folds of her wrap she brings out the pages of parchment. She pulls the cord that holds the scroll together. Across the pages are the small ink strokes of the Arabic script. She holds the parchment to her nose and smells the dark murkiness of the ink. She doesn't have to read the words. She knows the story so well. It is written on her heart.

They said the wave that struck her grandfather had been of gigantic proportions. It had struck while he stood on the crumbling limestone sea wall of Kilwa. Onlookers had said that the peculiar thing about the wave was that it had come not as a single straight line, but rather that it had welled up out of the sea as an enormous hump. Like the back of a gigantic turtle.

And that the old man had raised his arms towards the wave and with a sigh it had taken him.

When the news was brought to their house, her grandmother and her grandmother's brother, who was her great-uncle, had not seemed at all surprised by this report. They had listened and then smiled at each other and merely nodded.

And later her grandmother had given her the scrolls of parchment wrapped with the red silken thread. 'This is the story of your grandfather's journey.'

Then her great-uncle had placed on her thumb the silver ring with its stones of brilliant cornelian and dark lapis lazuli. 'This belonged to your grandfather and his father before him. Your grandfather wasn't wearing it this morning when he walked along the sea wall. It lay next to his journal on a piece of parchment with your name written on it.'

Now she removes the heavy ring from her thumb and holds it up to the lamplight. The cornelian glows as fiery red as the inside of a pomegranate. And the lapis lazuli is as dark as a deep, secret pool. She turns it slowly to examine the arabesques of silver scrollwork that interlock over the shank. Under the collar, which holds the stones, she traces a Persian script with the words: May it End Well.

She slips the ring back over her thumb so that its secret message is clasped against her skin. Then she looks down at the parchment pages filled with the curved faded strokes of her grandfather's writing and whispers the first sentence out loud so that the words will be sucked into the soft coral-stone walls of his courtyard.

'The mystery of wood is not that it burns but that it floats.'

Glossary

bao	game played with pebbles or seeds in hollows carved on a wooden board or in hollows in the ground (Swahili)
bere	hyena (Shona)
boma	a fort or an enclosure made with interwoven branches (Swahili)
chapungu	bateleur eagle (Shona)
dhow	sailing vessel with three-cornered lateen sails (Arabic)
donje	unprocessed cotton (Shona)
Dzimba Dzemabwe	Houses of stone (Shona)
hakata	divining dice, usually of bone (Shona)
hanga	guinea fowl (Shona)
haya kwa heri	farewell (Swahili)
hoto	African hornbill (Shona)
hungwe	fish eagle (Shona)
hwari	francolin or African partridge (Shona)
ingwe	leopard (Shona)
ishwa	termite or white ant (Shona)
jahazi	very large ocean-going dhow (Swahili)
jee	playful (Shona)

KiSwahili	the language spoken by the people living along the East coast of Africa. It comes from the Arab word 'sawahil' which means 'coast'.
la	no (Swahili)
maji	water (Swahili)
m'bira	musical instrument of metal strips tied over a dry gourd (Shona)
mufudzi	cattle-herder (Shona)
mukonikoni	dragonfly (Shona)
mukwa	kiaat or bloodwood tree (Shona)
mupfura	tree bearing fruit that elephant especially enjoy commonly called 'marula' (Shona)
mupani	type of tree with brilliant orange foliage in autumn (Shona)
mupuma	combretum or wild willow tree (Shona)
muroyi	witch (Shona)
musimbiti	ironwood tree (Shona)
mutoriro	flute made of hollow reed with stop-holes and sealed at both ends (Shona)
muunga	umbrella-shaped African acacia thorn tree (Shona)
Mwari	God, Creator or Supreme Spirit (Shona)
N'anga	man who divines by throwing dice (Shona)
ndatenda	thank you (Shona)
nungu	porcupine (Shona)
shavi-shavi	red-billed hoopoe (Shona – also means butterfly)

Shona	the ethnic group and language of Bantu-speaking people who moved from Central Africa southwards to the area known as Zimbabwe today.
tzoko	vervet monkey (Shona)
tzinza	oribi – type of antelope (Shona)
uroyi	witchcraft (Shona)
Zanj	coast of the blacks (Arabic)